T. R. Barkley doesn't
Amy Travis.

He watched Amy walk away from him to where she had dropped her saddle. It wasn't the light, narrow, cavalry-issue saddle the men used. It was made from soft reddish leather with intricate tooling. He wondered if she had brought it from Albany or if the major had bought it for her somewhere. She untied her bedroll and spread the dark wool blanket on the ground before she lay down with her head on the saddle and the horse's blanket. It was getting cold. She ought to have something warmer to wear, but the wool blanket beneath her would help.

He went to his gear. Buck's saddle blanket was damp, and he had spread it out to air. He untied the leather thongs that held his own blanket to his saddle and shook it out, then walked over to her, carrying it over his arm.

She was already turned on her side with her eyes closed. He draped the blanket over her gently. Her eyes came open, and she stared up at him.

"Thank you," she whispered.

"It's nothing." He turned away, confused by the feelings that were unbalancing him. He wanted to protect her from more than hostile Indians. He wanted to keep her safe forever.

He went to his saddlebags and took out his second shirt. It was a warm blue flannel, and he put it on over his other shirt, then lay down, pillowing his head on the saddlebags.

He was getting soft. Maybe he would have done the same for his sister. More likely, Rebecca would have taken his blanket without asking. He wondered what Amy Travis would look like with her golden hair uncoiled.

SUSAN PAGE DAVIS and her husband, Jim, have been married twenty-eight years and have six children, ages ten to twenty-six. They lived in Jim's home state of Oregon for a time, then moved to Maine, where Susan grew up. They are active in an independent Baptist church. Susan began writing fiction as a child, when she also developed a love of history, horses, and reading. As an adult she was busy for many years homeschooling their children and writing news and other nonfiction, including some teaching materials for homeschool use. She later resumed fiction writing and began publishing short stories in 2001 in the romance, humor, and mystery fields. This is her first published novel, and she would love to hear from readers.

Protecting Amy

Susan Page Davis

Heartsong Presents

To our adventurous daughter, the real Amy, who went West and found true love with her own "T.R."

A note from the Author:
I love to hear from my readers! You may correspond with me by writing:

Susan Page Davis
Author Relations
PO Box 719
Uhrichsville, OH 44683

ISBN 1-59310-124-4

PROTECTING AMY

Our mission is to publish and distribute inspirational products offering exceptional value and biblical encouragement to the masses.

All Scripture quotations are taken from the King James Version of the Bible.

All of the characters and events in this book are fictitious. Any resemblance to actual persons, living or dead, or to actual events is purely coincidental.

PRINTED IN THE U.S.A.

Or check out our Web site at www.heartsongpresents.com

one

"Get my daughter out of here." Major Travis's words came out tight and stark, and T. R. Barkley eyed him silently.

As a civilian scout for the army, Barkley was used to being ordered around, but this time was different. The major was nervous, and with good reason.

"I'll give you two men. I can't honestly spare them, but you've got to get her through to Fort Laramie." Travis swung around and faced him, the cords on his uniform fluttering.

"Sir, I'll get through faster with your message if I go alone."

"You've got to take Amy," Travis insisted, his blue eyes adamant. "Nothing good is going to happen here. You know that."

Barkley lowered his gaze. He had just come in from three weeks of reconnoitering, and he did know. He'd informed the commanding officer himself. The Indians were gathering, making tentative peace among tribes who were traditional enemies. The tribes that had traded freely at the fort had become sullen and hostile, but until Barkley confirmed it, Travis had not believed they would make a concerted attack with the aim of removing the white man's garrison from Fort Bridger. Barkley had made the best count he could, gathered every scrap of information, then hurried back to the fort.

"Might be best to just pull back," he suggested.

"Abandon the fort?" Travis paced angrily to the window that looked out on the parade ground. "I have orders, Barkley. The government just bought this fort from civilians and made it a military installation. It's taken a lot of effort to bring it up to our standards. Washington would not be happy if I gave it up within months of establishing the outpost here. I'm to

5

hold this position no matter what."

The scout ran his hand through his beard. "No offense, Major, but those orders were written a long time ago by men who had no clear view of the situation."

Travis's eyes narrowed. He was near retirement, Barkley guessed. Fifty, at least. The word around the barracks was that if the major could hold Fort Bridger for a year, they'd discharge him honorably with a pension. And he'd done that for eight months, but the way Barkley saw it now, the major had little chance of living out the week.

"Get Amy away from here tonight," Travis demanded. "You know it's her best chance. If she stays here. . ." He didn't need to say more. His eyes pleaded.

Barkley nodded in resignation. "All right, as soon as it's dark. Give her a good horse, and tell her to pack light."

"Thank you. I won't forget this."

Barkley could only hope the man wouldn't have a tragic reason to remember and regret.

He left the major's office and went out the gate to the bank of the Black Fork. There wasn't time to go home. He'd bathe in the river and shave here, then sleep for a few hours in the barracks. When dusk fell, he would be in the saddle again.

But this time he wouldn't be creeping alone toward the Indian camps, outfoxing the foxes to learn their ways. He'd be flying toward Fort Laramie with a desperate call for reinforcements and with Travis's precious daughter.

He didn't like it. Travis ought not to have brought her here in the first place. Fort Laramie was one thing, but Fort Bridger was a small post three hundred and fifty miles to the west and had no amenities. The wives of two other officers had come out in April for two months' visit, but they had left eight weeks ago. Travis, a widower, had brought his youngest daughter out. He'd been away from home nearly a year and craved his family. But he should have sent her back to Laramie when the other women went.

Barkley rarely saw Amy Travis. He only went to the fort when the major needed him. He had a cabin five miles away, where he lived alone. He'd been only a boy when his family came with one of the first wagon trains through the Green River Valley in 1845. His mother became very ill on the trail, and when they arrived at Jim Bridger's trading post, his father decided to stop right there, in Indian territory, and build a homestead within a few miles of the post, or the fort, as Jim Bridger styled it. Bridger himself was still at the fort then, and Barkley's father became friends with the legendary mountain man.

The Indians generally had a good relationship with Bridger and clustered around the fort to trade. For several years, wagon trains heading for California and Oregon stopped there to rest and trade. Now they mostly bypassed Fort Bridger, taking a cutoff farther north, making directly for Fort Hall, but some still came this way, taking the Mormon Trail.

Somehow the Barkleys' homestead, hidden in a peaceful little valley, had been ignored by hostiles. T. R. Barkley thought Jim Bridger's proximity and rapport with the natives had protected his family, and for thirteen years they had lived unmolested. Once or twice his father had had problems with pilfering and had learned to lock up his stock and tools, but for the most part, the Barkleys were left alone. When Bridger sold the fort to the Mormons and moved on to bigger adventures, the climate had changed around the outpost.

Barkley's family had changed, too. His parents were dead now, and his sister, Rebecca, had married a lieutenant and gone east. His older brother, Richard, was dead; his horse had fallen on him. Young Matt had joined the army and was back at Fort Laramie. If he went to beg Major Lynde for troops to relieve Major Travis, chances were that Matt would be among them.

Returning to the fort after he'd washed himself, Barkley was leading his horse across the parade ground when a flash of color drew his eye. Amy Travis was coming out of the major's quarters, a small house under the wall of the fort. Her deep plum-colored skirt swirled around her as she walked quickly toward her father's office. It was hot, and she wore a white shirtwaist without the formality of a jacket. Her hair was hidden under a lavender bonnet. He'd never been close enough to see her eyes, but he guessed they were blue like her father's.

He'd heard she was a wild thing, always wanting to be out riding the prairie. Her father became exasperated, having to detail men to watch her. She was reputed to be a phenomenal horsewoman and a half-decent shot with a rifle. Barkley didn't know. He usually made a point of staying away from women.

He'd seen her once, across the parade ground, when a chaplain had passed through and held a worship service for the garrison. Amy Travis had sat demurely beside her father that day on one of the benches carried out from the mess hall. She kept her eyes downcast. He'd glimpsed her profile, solemn and earnest beneath the brim of her bonnet. He wasn't sure whether she was beautiful or not, but he liked the way she looked, and he knew she affected him in a way no other woman ever had. That disturbed him. He had stayed away from the fort for weeks afterward.

Which woman was the real Amy Travis? The subdued angel or the rash daredevil?

The sight of her now made him stop in his tracks. Two troopers walked past him, toward the barracks, momentarily blocking his view of her. How could they carry on with their routine while she was in sight? Maybe they feared her father's wrath, or maybe they were just used to her presence.

Miss Travis didn't look toward him, and he let his gaze linger as she walked. If she wasn't beautiful, she was striking at least. That uneasy feeling returned, but it wasn't unpleasant. Barkley felt a pang of regret as she disappeared through the door to her father's office.

"So, T.R., you're back."

He jumped and turned his head. Corporal Jim Markheim

was leaning on the doorjamb at the entrance to the barracks.

"Jim," Barkley said in acknowledgment.

"Just admiring the view?" Markheim asked with a chuckle.

Barkley felt his face warm beneath his tan, and he tugged at Buck's reins. He'd have enough time later to decide whether or not Amy Travis was pretty. He still didn't like taking her with him. She would slow him down and perhaps endanger his mission, but it seemed he had no choice.

"Can I get a shave around here?" he asked, looping Buck's reins around the hitching post and reaching for his saddlebag.

Markheim shrugged. "It's dry, T.R. Don't know as we'd ought to spare the water for a dirt clod like you."

"The well's dry?" Barkley asked. That would be bad news with the attack coming.

"No, I'm pulling your leg. The water level's low, but that well has never gone dry yet, so they say."

Barkley nodded. His older brother had helped dig that well seven years ago. The occupants of Fort Bridger could always get plenty of water from the Black Fork, but in the event of a siege, the well would be crucial.

He fingered the damp whiskers on his chin. "Well, I reckon I'll get shaved then."

"Better wash your clothes, too." Markheim held his nose and grimaced as Barkley pushed past him.

❧

"I won't go," Amy said flatly. She was annoyed to the edge of anger. She'd been separated from her father much of her life as the army sent him from one assignment to another, and she didn't want to leave him now.

He stood up, returning her glare. "Yes, you most certainly will. I was a fool to keep you here this long. It was selfish of me. Now I have to send three good men to make sure you make it safely to civilization."

"You don't need to do any such thing. I want to stay with you, Father."

"I've told you: The situation has deteriorated to the point where that is no longer possible."

"Do you honestly think they're going to attack the fort?"

"Yes, I do. Our civilian scout says they are, and he knows what's what when it comes to Indians."

"But surely you don't think those savages can overpower the fort? You can repulse them."

"It all depends." Her father frowned and studied the map on the wall behind his desk.

"On what?" Amy stepped closer to him. His gravity was beginning to worry her. She'd never before heard him suggest that his outfit might not survive an Indian attack.

"On how many there are of them and how soon we can get reinforcements."

"You're asking Major Lynde for reinforcements from Fort Laramie?" The garrison at Fort Bridger was only fifty men strong at the moment, hardened cavalry troopers. Most had served at Fort Laramie or one of the other western forts before being assigned at Bridger, but still, fifty men seemed inadequate, Amy thought, if an attack was likely.

"Yes. I'm sending Barkley. He'll take you with him and deliver you to Mrs. Lynde. From there, you can go back to your sister in Albany. If things go well here, I'll send you word. If not. . ."

"Daddy." She never called him *Daddy,* except when she was frightened. It had slipped out, and she saw when he looked at her that he knew she was afraid now.

"I'm sorry, Amy. The truth is, if we don't get reinforcements fast, things could go badly. I don't like to frighten you, but there are times when you ought to be afraid."

Amy sat down hard on her father's oak chair. She was a tomboy, a daring, fearless girl, or so the boys at home had thought. She would walk a fence rail or ride a bucking mule or jump off the bridge over Walker Stream. In reality, she was scared out of her mind to do any of those things, but she'd felt somehow that she couldn't let anyone see it. So she gritted her teeth and did them. After a while, taking risks had become a series of exciting adventures instead of terrifying ordeals.

Coming west had been the biggest adventure of all. Since her mother had died, she'd lived with her married sister, Elaine, but when their father was selected as the first commanding officer at Fort Bridger, he sent word that she might join him if she wished.

If she wished! It was wonderful! Elaine had fretted about her traveling alone, but Amy had gone off by stagecoach to Cincinnati and from there had joined the wife of a captain stationed at Fort Laramie. After two months of travel, she'd arrived at Fort Bridger exhausted. It had taken her a week to get her energy and high spirits back. Then her father had had his hands full trying to control her.

She knew she'd stretched his patience to the limit, but when the limit was in sight, she eased off and coddled him. He loved that. She mended his uniforms and brought him coffee at his desk in the middle of the morning. She baked the applesauce cake her mother used to make and knit him a pair of soft, black wool socks.

She stood up and put her hands on his shoulders, fussing with the epaulets. "You ought to have told me sooner."

"Maybe. I hoped we could smooth things over."

She straightened her shoulders, knowing there was only one thing she could do to ease his mind. "All right. I'll go, but only so you won't worry."

"Good girl." He leaned over and kissed her forehead. "You'd just be in the way here."

"You've got to be careful, Father."

He laughed ruefully. "Oh, don't worry about me. I'll sell this fort dearly. And if Barkley gets to Laramie in good time, I may have reinforcements before the hostiles make a move."

She nodded, determined not to impede the scout's progress. "There's one thing, though, Father. Please don't make me go back to New York. I'll wait at Fort Laramie, and when it's over, you send for me, and I'll come back."

"Oh, Amy—"

"Please? I've loved being with you. I don't want to give that up."

Her father's eyes were troubled. "I thought it was safe when I brought you here."

"It was. We had a wonderful time together this spring, didn't we, and most of the summer?"

He nodded. "We'll see, my dear."

"Good. I'll wait at Laramie."

"But you must promise to behave, girl. Don't give Major Lynde the headaches you've given me."

She laughed. "I won't. His wife will keep me busy, trying to match me up with the single officers. That's what she did when I came out."

"If only you'd settle down," Travis said in mock exasperation. "I think it will take quite a man to handle you, Amy Margaret."

"Someday, Father."

"Yes. There's plenty of time. Now, you listen to me. Barkley says you must travel light. You're to leave most of your things here. Wear your riding skirt, and take one change of clothing. I'll send the rest of your things when it's safe."

"That old scout said all that? I didn't know he could talk." She laughed, but her father's eyes narrowed.

"You'd be surprised what T. R. Barkley can say when he has a reason to speak. And listen to me, girl. When he tells you something on the trail, you pay attention. He won't waste words, but he knows this territory, and your life is in his hands."

She swallowed and smiled weakly. "Yes, sir. I'll be good."

Travis's eyes softened. "He's a good man, honey. He'll get you through. Now, I've got the supply sergeant packing for you and the escort, other than your personal things. And Amy. . ." He looked keenly at her. "You must promise me you'll take care of Kip."

"Father! You're letting me take Kip?" The joy that spurted up in her was tempered by the realization that he was giving her the swift, valiant horse for a reason. He honestly believed she would be in danger.

"Nothing but the best for you, dear, but don't run him into a chuckhole."

She threw herself into his arms.

"I'll keep him safe for you at Fort Laramie, Father. And I'll be safe, too. When the troops come from Laramie, you'll know I'm all right."

two

Barkley stood on the catwalk at the top of the fort's wall, watching the sun go down behind the massive, forbidding mountains to the west. There were wispy clouds, not the serious kind that would bring a soaking rain to the parched land, but enough to splinter the rays of light into glorious color. He watched until the last bits of rose and lavender were swallowed up in the gray of the evening sky and turned toward the ladder. Time to move.

His buckskin gelding was saddled and waiting. Buck wouldn't win any prizes for beauty, but he was sturdy and strong. Half quarter horse and half mustang, Buck was fast, and he didn't know when to quit. Barkley gathered the reins and led him toward the commanding officer's quarters.

Major Travis was saying good-bye to his daughter, and Amy was listening earnestly.

Should have sent her out two months ago, Barkley thought again. Now it was up to him to get her safely to Fort Laramie. Four days' hard ride, if they were lucky. He hoped it wouldn't take longer. Travis would need Major Lynde's troops soon.

She kissed her father one last time, and Jim Markheim led up her horse. Barkley recognized the rangy gray as one of the major's three personal mounts. He was big and fast, and the major thought a lot of him. Good. He recognized the precariousness of the flight and was giving Amy his best horse.

Barkley looked over the two troopers Travis had detailed to go with him. It must have been a difficult decision. Send two sharpshooters to protect his daughter when he'd need every gun he could lay hands on? He'd chosen two privates. Barkley recognized Layton by sight but knew nothing about him. He

14

was short, wiry, and alert. Brown was taller, slouching lazily in the saddle, but Barkley knew he'd be full of action when the need came. He was a decent tracker, a fair shot, and stubborn as all get-out. Barkley was glad Travis had picked him.

Amy Travis put her boot in the stirrup. Her father gave her a little boost as she swung onto the gray's back, then led the horse to where Barkley and the troopers were waiting.

"Amy, you've met our scout, T. R. Barkley."

"Not really," she said, looking him up and down.

Barkley touched the brim of his hat. "Ma'am."

"He'll get you where you're going." Travis said it as if he were taking Amy across the street to visit a neighbor.

She nodded. Her golden hair was up, hidden under a soft brimmed hat, not one of the calico bonnets he'd seen her wear around the fort. In the twilight, he couldn't tell if she'd inherited the blue eyes or not.

"You take care," the major said sternly.

"I will, Daddy."

Travis looked keenly at Barkley, and he nodded. They'd already settled things. Travis had seen that they had food, blankets, water, a little hard money, ammunition. Barkley knew the dire consequences if he failed in his twofold mission. Nothing remained to be said.

The scout mounted and turned Buck toward the trail, not looking back. He heard the other three horses following closely. He wanted to put a lot of miles between them and Fort Bridger before the half-moon rose at midnight.

They rode without speaking, with Barkley ten yards ahead of the others. Amy Travis came next on the long-legged gray, and the two troopers rode behind her.

Barkley knew the gray gelding could outrun Buck, but Amy kept him back, allowing him to concentrate on the trail ahead. They trotted briskly up the valley, paralleling the Black Fork, heading for the Green River. As they approached the pass, they rode high above the river, on a winding trail that rose between the looming peaks. Barkley kept Buck in the ground-eating trot the horse could sustain for hours, heading east.

To his left, the ground dropped away to the wide, slow-moving stream, which in August was shallow and sluggish. Clumps of trees grew near its banks, and the dark tops of some of those trees were as high as the level they rode on. He knew that when they left the mountains, trees would be scarce for the rest of the journey. When wagon trains reached Bridger, the emigrants always commented on the trees and the acres of green grass in the lush valley. It was a relief to eyes that had seen only the open prairie for weeks, with brown grass, dried and brittle by the time the weary oxen limped into the haven.

After three hours, they left the Black Fork and cut across several miles of open ground to the Green River. The bank cut down sharply in front of them. Barkley knew the best place to cross the stream and angled Buck along the edge until he came to the most gradual slope in the bank. He slowed his horse for the descent and heard the others close behind him.

When they reached the bottom, he dismounted and took Buck's bridle off, turning him loose to drink.

Layton and Brown followed Amy down to the edge of the water. Brown snapped a line around his mare's neck before removing her bridle, but Layton let his bay drink with the bit still in his mouth.

Amy rode the big gray close to where Barkley stood. She seemed able to handle the horse, but he didn't want any problems.

"Will that horse come to you?" It was the first time he had spoken to her, really. Her nearness triggered his pulse, and the question came out more gruffly than he'd intended.

She hesitated. "I'm not sure. Kip always comes to Father, but I don't know as I dare turn him loose out here. I have hobbles, though."

She held the reins slack as she hopped lightly down and

opened the saddlebag on the near side. Barkley fought the impulse to jump to her side and offer to take care of the task. Better to let her be as independent as possible. He turned to Brown.

"We'll stop twenty minutes and give the horses a breather."

"All right. Seems like a quiet night."

"So far."

The starlight was enough to show where a gravel bar spread halfway across the stream. Barkley walked out on it, then waded the rest of the way over. The water wasn't more than two inches deep. On the other side, he picked up the path and climbed the bank. At the crest, he could look out over the prairie for a mile or more, toward the eastern ranges of the Rockies, where the moon was rising, just pushing above the horizon, big and yellow. The tough grasses waved in a light breeze that at last relieved the heat of the day.

If they could move along undisturbed for another four hours, they would be well on the way to South Pass, although they would still be within hostile territory. He would stop at daybreak to let Miss Travis rest while he scouted the trail ahead as far as the pass. He knew the danger would not be at an end until they were safe inside the walls of Fort Laramie.

He could hear the river, the gurgling swirl of water over the rocks. He could hear the horses, too, pulling grass and snorting below him. He heard her footsteps long before she had toiled up the bank.

He knew it was Amy without turning around. Her skirt made a swishing sound that no man's clothing ever made. He realized she was trying to be quiet, and truthfully, she wasn't all that noisy, but it was a different sound that stood out in the silence of the night as much as the champing of the horses.

When she was nearly beside him, she scuffled a bit, and he thought she might have lost her footing, but he didn't turn and reach out to her. A moment later, she stood next to him, breathing a little fast.

He kept still, looking out at the way they would take. The moon had slowly separated itself from the edge of the earth and sprung above it, smaller and whiter now.

Amy's breathing slowed and grew quieter, and he thought she was purposely bringing it under control. She stood beside him, looking and waiting. He wondered if she expected him to say something, but he couldn't think of anything worth breaking the silence for.

"Mr. Barkley," she said at last. It was little more than a whisper.

He turned toward her. She had removed the felt hat and held it down at her side. Her hair was burnished gold in the moonlight. In the daytime, she had better keep it well covered, Barkley thought. She wore a dark blouse, not the white one he'd seen her wearing earlier. He was glad; the deep brown cotton wouldn't reflect the moonlight.

"How well do you know my father?" she asked.

He looked off east again, thinking about that. He had met Travis perhaps a dozen times over the last eight months at the fort or out on the plains. They had camped together a couple of times when he rode with one of the major's detachments. They had talked most of those times about the Indians and the land and the life in the West. But they weren't friends exactly.

He respected Benjamin Travis. The major had come into the fort with authority but without arrogance. He was willing to learn from others with more experience in the territory, and he seemed fair where his command was concerned. He'd taken on the difficult tasks of rebuilding the fort and keeping the tension with the Mormon pioneers at a minimum. Barkley found nothing about Major Travis to criticize.

⁂

The scout was silent so long that Amy wondered if he had heard her. She felt suddenly very exposed, and she knew she would be frightened out here so far from the fort and her father if this man weren't standing so solid and competent beside her.

"Don't know him real well," Barkley said at last. It was loud enough to carry to her ears but no farther. "I've worked with him some."

Amy looked at the scout's profile. He was handsome, perhaps rendered more so by the moonlight that softened his features. He wasn't scruffy looking; he had shaved that day, she was sure. He wore a dark shirt and pants, not the smelly buckskins she had seen on the shaggy scouts at Fort Laramie. He was young. It had startled her back at Fort Bridger when she'd first seen him up close. He seemed to have years and years of frontier living behind him and intimate knowledge of the Indians' customs and habits, but he was still in his mid-twenties, she was sure now.

He hadn't come to any of the social gatherings at the fort last spring. She'd seen him only occasionally, silently flitting in and out of the fort, but she hadn't really noticed him. He was another man among dozens at the fort, a part of the scenery. Until today, she had vaguely supposed he was one of those feral mountain men who couldn't read but knew every beaver lodge between here and Canada.

Now he was very important to her, and she wanted to know why her father had entrusted her to this particular man, the quiet young scout who crept around in the brush for weeks, watching the Indians for him. It occurred to her that the safety she had enjoyed on her rides near the fort might somehow be connected to this man.

"My father seemed a bit fatalistic today." Even her quiet voice was loud in the stillness. He looked quickly at her, and she said more softly, "He's never been that way before."

"Your father's a good man. He knows what he's doing."

"Do you think—is he really in danger?"

"Always in danger out here, ma'am."

She shivered. If her father was in danger inside Fort Bridger, how much danger were they in out here, unprotected? But her father wouldn't have sent her away if he'd thought she would be safer with him.

"We'd best move," Barkley said quietly. He turned and went down the path, waiting for a moment at the stream bank until she had climbed safely down but not holding his hand out to aid her. As soon as her feet were on the level ground at the bottom, he turned and waded into the shallow stream, toward the gravel bar. She followed, trying to keep her leather boots from splashing in the water.

Brown was watching the grazing horses, keeping an eye on the path they had come by. As they walked across the gravel bar, Layton went to the big gray and began bridling him for Amy, then stooped to remove the hobbles.

Barkley gave a low whistle, and his buckskin walked eagerly toward him. Amy watched him rub the gelding's forelock, then reach for the bridle that he'd looped over the saddle horn. He never wasted a motion, and he slipped the bit easily between the buckskin's teeth.

"All set, ma'am," Layton said.

She walked to Kip's side. The stirrup was high on the tall gelding's side, and Layton's hand came under her elbow, giving her a little leverage as she sprang up onto Kip's back. The private was being attentive, and Amy wondered if she ought to let him know somehow that she wasn't getting personal with any man just now. There was nothing offensive in his manner yet. He might just be more gentlemanly than Brown or Barkley, might have been raised to offer more assistance to ladies. She decided to ignore it for now.

❧

The breeze had found its way into the riverbed, and the tree-tops ruffled and stirred.

Barkley wanted to get out of the ravine. He couldn't hear all the tiny sounds he wanted to with the trees tossing and the stream trickling. He mounted Buck and pushed him across the water, then up the far bank. At the top, he moved out far enough so the others could gain the high ground without running into Buck, then halted and listened and looked. Nothing seemed to have changed. He glanced over his shoulder. Amy had stopped Kip just behind him and was stroking the gray's neck where the black mane fell on the left side. Behind her, Layton and Brown were waiting, their horses sidestepping nervously.

He lifted his reins just a hair, and Buck moved into his trot. Behind him, the other horses picked up the pace and came on steadily.

They rode over the silver-washed hills for hours, dark silhouettes against the ever-swaying grass. Barkley's lips were dry. The wind would be stinging the tender skin of Amy Travis's face, he was sure, but he couldn't help her except to maintain the pace and get her closer to Fort Laramie before the sun rose.

An hour before dawn, he halted Buck suddenly, raising his hand to slow the riders behind him. Before him, the tall grasses lay down in a straight line from the trail they followed toward the river on his left. It was not a worn, well-beaten track, but the trail of several animals that had recently passed that way.

The other horses came up close, and he motioned to Brown. The trooper rode up beside him and silently surveyed the scene, then looked toward the river.

Amy hung back a little, and Layton kept his horse beside hers. Barkley shot a glance at Brown.

"Reckon we ought to check it out?" Brown asked softly.

"You go on," Barkley told him. "Move out away from the river a little. I'll have a look and catch up. Keep Miss Travis between you. If you find some cover, wait for me."

Brown nodded and rode back to where Layton and Amy sat on their mounts. Almost immediately they moved out, away from the flattened grass, continuing east. Barkley moved

Buck into the trail and walked him slowly toward the river. Twenty yards from where the land descended sharply, he stopped. There was no cover for the horse; he would have to leave him there. He turned Buck off the trail into the tall grass, dismounted, and tugged down on the reins.

Buck snuffled quietly, then lay down. After petting the horse, Barkley went back to the path. Buck's hiding place would not fool a tracker, but he would not be in plain sight to anyone approaching as the sun rose.

The scout crouched low and crept swiftly toward the river. He could hear it above the wind now. It was wide and low along this stretch, swirling around rocks. He gained the edge of the embankment and stared down into the bottom of the wide draw. The flat, dark water lay before him with the moonlight on it, and willows crowded the brim. And yes, horses grazed down there. He counted seven. Two were pintos, with large splotches of white clearly visible. There was no campfire, no smoke.

At last he made out dark spots under the trees. He thought they must be people stretched out to sleep. He wished he could get nearer, but he didn't dare, not with Amy Travis to protect. He was more than half certain they were Indians, and even then they might be friendly, but the way things had been going lately, they probably were not.

There might be a guard on duty. Barkley sat for several minutes, watching for any movement, any gleam or any dark spot that was not still. There was so much motion already with the restless horses, the flowing water, and the tossing treetops that it was hard to be sure.

Finally he turned away, satisfied, and went stealthily back to where Buck lay. He threw his leg over the saddle and clucked, and Buck heaved to his feet, his head going up first, then his hindquarters. The two of them stood immobile as Barkley looked and Buck sniffed, then they headed for the track Amy and the troopers had followed.

He kept the horse at a quick walk for a quarter mile, then urged him into the extended trot. Daylight would be on them soon. He'd have to find a place where they could guard Amy and rest part of the day. They might need to lie low and wait for darkness if hostiles were on the move.

He thought of Major Travis and his urgent situation. It wouldn't be good to wait out the entire day. Travis needed those reinforcements.

Barkley hated being in this position, having to decide what was best or least dangerous for all concerned. Hide the daughter for the daylight hours or move on to get the aid the garrison needed? It would be different if he only had to worry about himself.

He realized suddenly that it wasn't his decision alone. There was always someone who had better foresight than he did. His mother had taught him as a child to take his problems to God. As he rode, Barkley began to pray in earnest for wisdom and for Amy Travis's safety.

Far ahead he saw the dark bulk of a line of trees, and he let Buck quicken his pace. They would be waiting there for him. It might have made a good stopping place for the daylight hours if it weren't so close to the party he'd just seen. They would definitely have to put some more ground between them before they stopped for another rest. If one of the natives rode up out of the river bottom to check on their back trail, the track of the four riders would be obvious.

He slowed Buck as he neared the trees and watched cautiously ahead. He didn't like riding into cover from the open like this.

The trees were between him and the rising sun, but even so, the gray light of early dawn showed him clearly where their horses had passed. He followed the trail of bent grass, watching the verge of the woods. When Barkley drew within ten yards, Brown stepped from between two cottonwoods and stood silently waiting for him. As soon as Barkley was close, the trooper turned and walked into the trees. Barkley followed.

A stream flowed through the copse toward the river, and the three horses were browsing on grass and leaves. Layton and Amy were seated, and Barkley dropped Buck's reins and walked toward them. Brown stood beside him.

"Indians," Barkley reported. "At least seven horses. I couldn't tell much without getting closer than I liked. I think we'd best move on."

"Sun's coming up," Layton said.

"Yes, but our trail's too plain."

"Reckon we ought to stick with the wagon trail?" Brown asked quietly.

Barkley nodded. "Our tracks will be less obvious. Sandy Creek flows into the river up ahead. We'll follow it northeast for thirty miles or so, then we'll have a stretch of twenty-five miles along the Little Sandy to South Pass."

"All right," said Brown.

"We'll stop and rest and water the horses when we get to Little Sandy Creek if we don't run into any problems on the way. I'd like to keep riding until then." Barkley turned his eyes on Amy. "How about it, Miss Travis? Can you ride another thirty miles before we rest again?"

"I'm fine," she said, but he knew she must be tired. She had pluck.

"You hungry?"

"I can wait."

He couldn't help smiling. They'd been riding all night, and she must be starved. His own stomach was crying out for breakfast, even though he was used to going long stretches between meals.

"Layton, get out something we can chew on."

The trooper took biscuit and dried beef from his packs, and they sat eating a cold breakfast while Brown watched the trail behind them, beyond the trees. Barkley wished they had hot coffee, but they couldn't risk a fire.

"You all set, Miss Travis?"

She looked up at him. The sun had risen, and even in the shade of the trees, the blue of her eyes was startling. Odd how his heart hammered when he noticed them. He didn't like it. It made it hard to concentrate on their purpose.

"I'm ready anytime you are, Mr. Barkley."

He was seeing an unexpected side of her—not the unmanageable tomboy, not the submissive daughter. She seemed to be maturing under his eyes.

Barkley cleared his throat. "You must be tired, but I think we'd best not stick around here too long."

A saucy smile crept out as she stood up and brushed off her brown skirt. "If I fall asleep in the saddle, don't let me fall off and be left behind."

He couldn't help returning the smile. "Don't worry, ma'am. I'll tie you in the saddle if need be."

three

An hour later, Barkley spotted smoke in the east—just a thin column from a campfire—and he was sure it was at a stopping place in the trail beside the creek.

Amy rode up beside him, letting the gray stretch his legs.

"Someone's up ahead?" she asked tentatively.

He nodded. "Probably an emigrant train camped there last night and hasn't got rolling yet."

They rode side by side, and he found himself snatching glances at her. Her golden hair was up under the hat, and she wore no adornments. She had an interesting face, he thought. Pretty, but more than that, full of curiosity about her surroundings. She could hardly wait to see what they would find at the campsite where the smoke rose and disappeared into the blue August sky.

They came to the place where the approach to the creek had been worn down by many wagon wheels. Barkley took Buck to a vantage point on the bank above for an overview of the low camp.

A train of eleven wagons circled loosely among the trees by the river. He squinted and frowned at the scene. The smoke came from only one campfire and people were moving about it, but they were moving too slowly to be preparing to travel.

"What is it?" Amy asked, watching his face rather than the camp below.

"Unless their cattle are farther downriver, some are missing. They don't have enough oxen there to haul those wagons."

She turned back to the scene laid out below and studied it. He saw her eyes flare as she took in the dozen oxen grazing inside the circle of wagons, a sprinkling of saddle horses among them. The women tending kettles at the fire or washing clothing in the river didn't seem alarmed, however. He could see only two men, and both held rifles. They stood near the wagons, looking back toward the wagon road.

"What does it mean?" Amy asked.

"Come on."

Barkley wheeled his buckskin and rode for the wagon trail. As the four horses approached the camp, heads went up. The two men with guns stiffened and trained their weapons on them, but Barkley raised his hat and waved it, and they slowly lowered the rifles.

He rode in at a trot, and Amy kept pace on Kip, with the two troopers close behind.

"What happened?" Barkley asked shortly.

"Injuns," said a stout, dark-haired man. "They came tearing in here at dawn and drove off most of our stock. Got away with nigh thirty mules, eight oxen, and a few horses. Most of our men have gone after 'em."

"North?" Barkley asked, looking toward the stream.

"No, back south again, into them hills." The man nodded toward the slopes that rose, brown with dry grass.

"Anyone hurt?" Barkley asked.

"One boy took an arrow in the leg," the man said. "It happened so fast, we didn't really have much chance to defend ourselves." He kicked sheepishly at a stone on the ground. "Didn't expect this to happen. Heard the tribes had been quiet lately."

"The boy all right?" Barkley asked.

"He'll mend."

"Show me the arrow."

The man did not question his authority but turned and headed for one of the wagons.

The second man, who was older, stood looking at the riders, and women and youngsters began to gather.

"You with the cavalry?" the old man ventured.

"Sort of. We're on the way to Fort Laramie," Barkley said.

"You been to Fort Bridger?" one of the women asked.

"Yes, ma'am." Barkley looked at the old man. "We saw a small band of Indians twelve or fifteen miles back. They didn't see us. But the tribes have been restless lately." He knew it was too far for these people to go back to Fort Laramie now. "You be alert between here and Bridger."

"How long will it take?" the old man asked. "I mean, if we get our mules back."

"Most a week with wagons, I reckon," Barkley said. Oxen would do well to make ten miles a day, he knew. He didn't like to think of the small band unprotected at this unsettled time.

The dark-haired man came back, holding a twenty-four-inch arrow with the tip cut off. Barkley reached for it and held it up, turning it thoughtfully.

"Lakota Sioux. How many men went after them?"

"Fifteen. Our horses were mostly tied up, so they only got three."

Barkley rubbed his chin. "I'd like to stop and help you, but I can't."

Layton eased his horse up on the other side of Amy's. "We'll tell the authorities at Laramie what happened," he said.

The two men nodded. "Tell them it's the Richardson party," the younger man said.

"How many Sioux?" Barkley asked.

"Seemed like a hundred," a tall, angular woman said.

"No, 'twarn't that many," the old man snorted. "They made an insufferable racket, but there warn't more than twenty of them."

Layton looked at Barkley.

"We can't," Barkley said. "Major Travis was explicit. We can't delay."

Layton crossed his wrists on his saddle horn and looked away.

"You got plenty of ammunition?" Barkley asked.

The young man nodded.

"Well, if you don't get your stock back, you pack everybody up and head for Bridger as quick as you can. Things are looking a mite uncertain just now."

He saw the fear leap into the women's eyes as they looked around quickly for their children. He didn't like to cause that, but neither did he like to think they might sit here for days or weeks in indecision.

He nodded to the emigrants and turned Buck back to the trail. He set a quick pace for the next hour despite the searing heat and was rewarded by the sight of the Little Sandy flowing into the larger stream.

He dismounted and led Buck down to the edge of the water, then unbridled him. While the gelding greedily slurped from the creek, Barkley squatted and removed his hat, dipping one hand in the water. It was very cold, even in mid-August, running down from the high peaks.

He saw Amy turn away Layton's offer of help as she struggled with the hobbles. When her horse was secure, she sat on a large rock and pulled off her tall leather boots.

He walked upstream a little ways, scouting for a likely spot for her to rest. The water was low, and there was a place where the ground beneath tall bushes beside the stream was dry and sandy. He ambled back toward the others.

Brown looked up as he approached, and Barkley beckoned to him. Brown was definitely the one to trust. The trooper came to him, and he said softly, "We'll stop here. You keep watch while I scout ahead a little."

Brown nodded.

"Tell the others to sleep, and keep an eye on the horses. There's a place yonder in the shade where Miss Travis can rest. When I get back, you rest and Layton can keep watch."

Brown gave him a curtailed salute.

Barkley almost told him not to light a fire and to watch the back trail, but he decided it was unnecessary to tell Brown that. It rankled him when people told him to do things he would do anyway, so he didn't say it.

He whistled for Buck, reluctant to take his mount away from the chance to graze, and rode out along the creek, following the deeply rutted trail. After half an hour, he sat and gazed long and hard eastward, toward South Pass, then turned and loped slowly back toward the others.

Brown stood up out of the grass as he approached. Barkley rode up close to him and dismounted.

"Miss Travis?" he said as he slipped the headstall over Buck's ears.

"She's asleep," Brown said with a grin. "Plopped down in the shade with her head on her saddle, and she was out."

Barkley smiled. "Layton?"

"Him, too. You'd best get a few winks yourself, T.R. I can stand another hour."

"All right, but no longer. We all need rest, and we'll need to be awake and alert."

The sun was high overhead when Layton woke him.

"Hate to do it," the private said.

Barkley was on his feet. He didn't feel truly rested, but he knew he could go on for some time now.

"Miss Travis still sleeping?"

"Like a baby." Layton's smile was smug, and Barkley felt annoyance. Had the trooper been watching her as she slept? He had been tempted to take a peek at her himself but had deliberately stayed away. He could see where she was stretched out on her blanket beneath the bushes, but he thought ladies needed their privacy.

"All right, see if you can get a little more rest." Barkley settled his hat comfortably on his head and walked to the stream, where he bent for a drink. At least they would have water most of the way.

He checked on the horses, then ambled up to where he could see behind them, down the almost imperceptible slope.

They would be heading upward faster now, climbing to the pass. It was hard work for the horses, but they were all in prime condition.

An hour later, he turned back toward the creek and walked quietly to where Brown lay leaning against a weathered log. He kicked the man's left boot gently.

Brown immediately opened his eyes and looked up at him, then stood, reaching for his rifle.

"Let's eat something and move," Barkley said, and Brown nodded.

Layton stirred, and Barkley knew he hadn't gone back to sleep. While Brown rummaged in the packs for food, Layton went to bring the horses closer.

Barkley stared after him thoughtfully. "How do you read Layton?" he asked Brown.

The trooper glanced up at him. "He's all right, I guess. Not my first choice in a pinch, but he's a good shot."

Barkley nodded. He walked slowly toward Amy. Her boots were set neatly beside her, and her stocking feet were drawn up to the hem of the loose divided skirt. She was curled on her right side, her face in the shade. She had folded Kip's woolen saddle blanket over the tooled leather seat of her saddle for a pillow, and her golden hair shone against the dull blue and black stripes of the blanket.

He stood just for the length of two short breaths, his pulse thudding in that disconcerting way. Softly, he said, "Miss Travis."

She didn't respond but breathed on steadily, and he envied her the sound sleep. Her face held a sweetness that caught at him and a vulnerability that brought home to him afresh the magnitude of his mission.

"Miss Travis—Amy," he said gently, leaning down to touch her elbow.

Her eyelids fluttered, and she looked up at him, startled for an instant, then sat up and reached for her boots.

He stood and walked to the log where Brown was rationing out cheese and biscuits. She seemed to know what to do without asking questions, and that pleased him. He was glad she wasn't a chatterbox and could perform simple tasks without detailed instruction. It made his job easier.

"You like working for the army?" Brown asked, handing him his food.

Barkley shrugged. "Travis is fair. Don't think I'd want to enlist, though."

Brown nodded. "I wish now I hadn't."

Barkley raised his eyebrows. "Why did you?"

"Things were really tough at home. We had a fire, lost everything. I took Martha and the boy to my folks', but they didn't really have room for us, and they're struggling, anyway. I figured if I did a year or two with the army, I could at least be sending my pay home. Martha's been putting by every cent she can, and we're hoping when I get home, we'll have enough to start over."

"I hope it works out for you."

Brown grimaced. "I've made up my mind. When I get home, I'm never leaving them again. Just between you and me, I miss them something fierce."

Barkley opened his canteen. "A man's allowed to miss his family."

Layton came to the log, and Brown gave him his ration.

Barkley looked over his shoulder and saw Amy standing up, pulling at the top of one boot, then stamping her foot a little. She stooped for the felt hat and perched it on her head, hiding the gleaming hair, and he took a deep, slow breath.

He turned away and saw that Layton watched her, too. Suddenly he felt foolish. He was an ordinary man, no different from any other. Perhaps she was an ordinary girl, and he only imagined she was special. How could he tell?

He walked toward the trail to eat while he kept watch once more.

Ten minutes later, Brown came up beside him, leading his chestnut mare, and Barkley relinquished his post to go saddle Buck.

The heat of the sun was scorching, and he kept the animals at a slow jog as they climbed the broad pass. The stream grew smaller as they went on, until it was a rivulet tumbling down its rocky course. The trail rose higher, and the air cooled.

Barkley always felt a thrill when he went over the pass. Somewhere ahead was the place he was born, still thousands of miles away. It seemed a foreign land to him: the East. Massachusetts. He could remember the farm there, the farms and shops and the church where the neighbors had gathered each Sunday. His father had kept sheep, and he and Richard had helped wash and shear them in the spring. He wasn't sure how much was really his memory and how much was the stories his parents had told.

He knew there were hundreds of towns close together with thousands of people in them. And they told him he had seen the ocean when he was a tyke, but that memory escaped him. He could remember ponds and a few large lakes but not the Atlantic. Jim Bridger had told his family about a huge salt sea he had seen to the west across the desert, but that, too, was out of Barkley's reckoning. Maybe someday he would go see it. Bridger told a lot of tales of the wonders he had seen, but so far Barkley hadn't caught the wanderlust. He liked the cabin in the mountains by the Black Fork.

Amy rode up beside him, the rangy gray stretching his legs, and again he wondered about her. She was reputed to be an adventurous girl, and she did seem to enjoy traveling. She hadn't complained, although the conditions were primitive. Her father had told him he was sending her back to the security of his married daughter's home. Was she ready to go back to Albany and sit in her sister's parlor, spinning yarn and embroidering runners?

She smiled when he looked at her, and his pulse quickened.

Yes, she had her father's eyes, but her mother must have been a beauty. Her smile lit her features with an enthusiasm that even the battered hat couldn't repress.

"We've left the creek," she said.

"Yes, this is the Continental Divide. We'll hit the Sweetwater soon—flowing east."

She nodded. "It's beautiful out here. I hope Father permits me to come back soon."

Barkley just hoped her father survived, and uppermost on his list of hopes right now was Amy's safety.

"He's right to send you away," he said.

"Even so, I'll miss it."

"Fort Bridger?"

"Yes. Well, everything." She stroked the horse's neck, leaning forward slightly, and the hat brim hid her features. "I'll miss Father, of course, and the feeling I have out here. There's freedom in the West."

He supposed that was true. A woman could do things here that she wouldn't be allowed to do in Albany or Boston. Wear a split skirt, for instance, and ride hundreds of miles in the company of three men. In Albany, she would probably ride sidesaddle or in a buggy and be closely chaperoned. She rode astride here without self-consciousness, and she sat easily in the saddle, even after so many hours. She held the reins lightly with her left hand, barely keeping the contact with Kip's mouth. Even his sister, Rebecca, wasn't the rider Amy Travis was.

"Do you miss anything from the East?" he asked.

"Well, yes," she admitted. "Father's library is quite meager. I suppose books are too heavy to cart all this way, and the traders don't bring any."

Barkley smiled. His own home held a shelf of well-worn books, and he, too, wished for more.

"What does your father have?" he asked.

"You mean besides army regulations and his Bible?"

"Yes. If I'd known, maybe I could have loaned you something."

"You have books?" Her face was animated, and he caught his breath. That look was for him.

"Just a few." He swallowed hard. "Do you have Franklin's autobiography?"

"No. Father has Calvin's *Institutes* and Edmund Burke and William Bradford, and an astronomy book. Oh, and Shakespeare. A volume of Woolman's sermons, too. That's the most of it, I think."

"Don't know Woolman," Barkley said, "but I wouldn't have suspected your father of reading sermons and law books."

Amy shrugged. "Father reads anything. He's wishing he'd brought more books along, too."

"Well, I have John Bunyan and David Brainerd and a volume of Milton's poetry. That was my mother's."

"Men can read poetry," she said with a stubborn note.

Barkley laughed. "Didn't say they couldn't. I've read it three or four times myself." *Milton would have loved her,* he thought. *"So lovely fair, that what seemed fair in all the world seemed now mean, or in her summed up, in her contained."* He looked away quickly, hoping she couldn't guess he was comparing her to Milton's Eve.

"If I do go back East, I'm going to send some more books to Father," she said. "One of the traders can fit a box of books in his wagon."

"It would be the first thing they'd toss out if they had trouble. You see things like that by the trail."

"Yes, I saw a lot of furniture this spring, coming out from Fort Laramie," Amy admitted. "Beautiful, some of it. Such a shame."

He nodded. "Once I saw a whole set of medical books. I'd have packed them home, but it would have been too much for Buck. Folks don't realize what they're facing when they leave Independence."

It struck him suddenly that he was talking more than he had in ages and was certainly having the most detailed conversation he had ever had with a woman.

"How long have you been out here?" she asked.

"Long time." He rode on, thinking about it and wondering if his father had traded away something precious for the open spaces of the West.

"Who taught you to read?" Amy asked.

He smiled. Her blue eyes were wide, and it was obvious she was surprised to find he was educated. "I had some school in Massachusetts, but my mother kept us all at it when we came. I was twelve when we settled out here."

"You were lucky," she said.

He'd never thought of it that way. It was what had happened, that was all. If they'd stayed in New England, perhaps his parents would have lived longer. Perhaps his brother Richard would still be alive. No, he wouldn't say lucky. But he was glad they had come, all the same.

A well-defined track veered off from theirs, almost straight west, while theirs came from the southwest. Barkley nodded toward it. "That's the cutoff. Most folks take that trail to Fort Hall now and don't come down to Bridger."

She nodded. Even for those heading for California, the cut-off was shorter. Fort Bridger was quite isolated as a result, though a few trains went that way, mostly Mormons headed for Utah. Trappers still frequented the outpost, but it hadn't grown into the thriving settlement Jim Bridger had envisioned.

Buck nickered softly, jerking Barkley's thoughts back to the present. "He smells water."

Amy's eyes glittered with subdued excitement, and he was glad she didn't need to chatter on. He was content to ride beside her without speaking for a while. There were things he'd ask her sometime, but not now.

They were descending an incline toward the river valley. The sun had dropped behind them, and the air had cooled noticeably.

"You cold?" he asked.

"A little."

"We'll stop soon, when we get to the Sweetwater, and let the horses graze."

She nodded.

Barkley looked behind him. Brown was five yards back, his horse ambling steadily along, while he looked off to the south, then behind them. Barkley was glad the private was alert. It was the first time he had let his mind wander from his purpose and let his vigilance lapse. He hadn't thought a woman's company would do that to him. Layton's bay was picking its path carefully, just behind Brown's horse. Layton was too far back for Barkley to read his expression, but he thought the trooper wasn't happy.

four

Amy swung stiffly from the saddle when they reached the bank of the Sweetwater. She tried not to let her fatigue show, but she was glad they were halting. She loved to ride, and having Kip as her mount was a joy, but Barkley's pace was wearing her out.

She unsaddled quickly and let Kip drink, then put the hobbles on him. Layton took up the guard's position, and Brown fussed over his mare's feet. She hoped there was no problem. She went to her saddle and untied her pack.

She was wishing she had brought her coat. She'd thought it would be too bulky and heavy for the horse to carry in the searing heat of the day, but the nights were chilly in the mountains. She took out the extra shirt she had packed and pulled it on over her brown blouse. It helped a little. She looked around, then scolded herself. She was searching for Barkley.

He came out of the shadows downstream and went to Brown, not looking her way. Amy tied her pack up again on the cantle of the saddle and made herself ignore the two men. Barkley was interesting, she admitted to herself, but she had met other interesting men. She had never lost her head over a man, or her heart. At the fort, she had cautioned herself about forming an attachment for any particular man and had managed to avoid that pitfall. Most of her father's officers were married, and she knew better than to show a preference for one of the enlisted men. She had remained impartial, but it hadn't been difficult, really. None of the men had impressed her as someone with whom she could happily spend the rest of her life.

So why was she being so silly about Barkley? As they rode, she watched his back. He rode straight but not stiff, at ease with Buck's movement. When they stopped, she kept track of him, trying not to let her eyes follow him. She felt safer when he was in sight.

And this afternoon she had risked riding Kip up beside his horse and striking up a conversation about books and freedom and civilization. She had been quite daring, she thought.

The man read Milton. She'd imagined him to be taciturn and illiterate, not an avid reader of poetry and classics. Had he and her father ever discussed books? Their relationship must be limited to business, but she had sensed a deep respect for Barkley when her father spoke of him. And Father had, after all, given her into the man's care. Competence and expertise were not enough. Ben Travis wouldn't entrust his daughter to any man who wasn't decent.

But Milton! The scout was far more complex than she had supposed.

Brown left his horse at last and came toward her.

"Best eat while we're stopped," he said.

"How long will we be here?"

"Probably an hour or two. T.R. wants to let the horses graze and rest a little, then we'll ride most of the night if you can stand it."

"We need to push on," she agreed. It had almost seemed like a picnic as she rode along with Barkley. Instead of trotting, the horses had walked down the incline, and the conversation had changed her entire view of the journey. For a while, it had become a pleasant outing, very pleasant, indeed. She felt quite the socialite, drawing out the reticent scout. But now reality was intruding again.

If her father and the fifty men at Bridger were to live, they must push onward relentlessly. It was that stark and simple.

"We'll keep an eye on your horse if you want to get a nap," Brown said.

"Thank you." Amy sat down on a rock and chewed her piece of jerky. Brown stood nearby, looking off toward the horses. "Is your mare all right, Private Brown?" she asked when she had swallowed.

"I think so. Thought she was favoring the off front foot for a while."

"Where are you from?" Amy asked. She thought she caught a strange flavor in his speech.

"Tennessee, ma'am."

Ah, he was a southerner. That was it.

"How long have you been out here?" she asked.

"Came to Fort Bridger when your father came. I was at Fort Kearney for a few months before that." The shadows were deepening, but Amy thought his face had a wistful air.

"Do you miss your home?"

"Oh, yes." It was deep and sure. "I hope to be going back East before too many more months."

"Oh? You have family in Tennessee?"

"Yes, ma'am." He hesitated, eyeing her from beneath the brim of his hat. "Got a boy back there, and my wife, and my folks."

"You're married?" It surprised her. She never thought much about the enlisted men's families.

"Oh, yes, ma'am," Brown said, and she thought he might have added, *Very married.*

"You miss them," she ventured.

"Yes, I surely do. I wasn't thinking to be so far from home for so long."

"You'll leave the army?"

"I believe I will, come January. Not the best time to travel in these parts, though. I've a mind to ask your pa to transfer me after this crisis is past."

"He'll do it."

"Oh, I don't know, Miss Travis. Privates get shuffled around where they're needed most."

"But you need to be with your family."

He was quiet again, and she wondered why he had joined up in the first place.

"How about Layton?" she asked. "Is he married, too?"

"Don't think so."

She didn't ask about Barkley. She was making an assumption that he was single, but it hit her at that moment that he, too, might be as married as Brown. He might even have an Indian woman stashed away in his cabin near the fort.

She glanced surreptitiously at Brown. Maybe she should ask, before she let herself think too much about T. R. Barkley. More and more he filled her thoughts. She had never been timid exactly, but this seemed too brazen. She realized she didn't care about Layton but had asked about him with a faint hope that Brown would enlighten her about Barkley's family, too.

She chewed the beef slowly. It made her thirsty, and she reached for the canteen that hung on her saddle. She walked to the edge of the river, stepped carefully out onto a flat rock, and stooped to fill the canteen. She would ask her father at the first opportunity to send Brown east of the Mississippi. He ought to be able to go straight home in January when he mustered out. Of course, there was all this talk about a possible war between the states. If that happened, she supposed Brown's loyalties would lie with the South. Hard to think of the faithful young soldier as a potential enemy. He'd served the United States Army well and would do his utmost to protect her now. She couldn't imagine him lining up opposite her father's troops.

She drank from the canteen and bent to top it off. She heard him come up behind her as she pounded the cork in with the heel of her hand. "Do you think there'll be a war?" she asked without turning around.

"I hope not."

She jumped and whirled around, nearly toppling off the

rock into the water. Barkley stood three feet from her in the twilight.

"I'm sorry, I thought you were Private Brown," she gasped.

"Didn't mean to startle you."

She was sure he was smiling.

"Oh, well, we'd been talking about homes and families and such, and he told me he's from Tennessee. I was thinking about what would happen if we went to war."

"Mm." Barkley seemed to ponder that. "Seems kind of far-fetched to me. We've got enough to worry about with the Indians. But I guess back East, folks are het up about it."

"Slavery, you mean?" she asked uncertainly.

"Oh, that and other things."

She'd heard some talk around the fort but did not consider herself well versed in the topic. It was a world away. Yet her father was a career army officer. If a war broke out before he retired, he would be in the thick of it. She felt suddenly bereft. The peaceful days with her father might be over regardless of the outcome of the situation at Fort Bridger.

She gathered her skirt to make the long step from the rock to the shore, and Barkley reached out to her, ready to steady her if she missed her footing. It surprised her. He'd never helped her with anything before. When she hopped lightly over, his hand settled on her wrist, and he pulled her quickly away from the edge, then let go.

"I'm hoping we can make Independence Rock by this time tomorrow. It'll be a hard ride." He looked intently at her, as if trying to gauge her endurance.

"All right." She felt the color rising in her cheeks. She told herself that the feelings of unswerving trust he aroused in her were because of her father's trust in him and because of the steadfastness she saw in him, but his touch had an astonishing effect on her. "That's halfway, isn't it?"

"Better than halfway. You'd best lie down for a while. We'll ride most of the night."

She nodded. "Just tell me when you want to move out."

૱

He watched Amy walk away from him to where she had dropped her saddle. It wasn't the light, narrow, cavalry-issue saddle the men used. It was made from soft reddish leather with intricate tooling. He wondered if she had brought it from Albany or if the major had bought it for her somewhere. She untied her bedroll and spread the dark wool blanket on the ground before she lay down with her head on the saddle and the horse's blanket. It was getting cold. She ought to have something warmer to wear, but the wool blanket beneath her would help.

He went to his gear. Buck's saddle blanket was damp, and he had spread it out to air. He untied the leather thongs that held his own blanket to his saddle and shook it out, then walked over to her, carrying it over his arm.

She was already turned on her side with her eyes closed. He draped the blanket over her gently. Her eyes came open, and she stared up at him.

"Thank you," she whispered.

"It's nothing." He turned away, confused by the feelings that were unbalancing him. He wanted to protect her from more than hostile Indians. He wanted to keep her safe forever.

He went to his saddlebags and took out his second shirt. It was a warm blue flannel, and he put it on over his other shirt, then lay down, pillowing his head on the saddlebags.

He was getting soft. Maybe he would have done the same for his sister. More likely, Rebecca would have taken his blanket without asking. He wondered what Amy Travis would look like with her golden hair uncoiled.

five

When Amy woke again it was dark. Stars glittered overhead, but the moon was nowhere to be seen. Layton had spoken to her and perhaps shaken her a little, but he moved away when she sat up. She looked around, realizing that the three men were all moving, preparing to leave. She rolled Barkley's blanket, and he came and took it wordlessly from her hands. She packed her own gear, then walked quickly downstream, looking for a private spot. Even without a mirror, she could tell her hair was disheveled.

When she came back a few minutes later, Layton was saddling Kip. She braided her long hair as she walked, quickly twisting the braid and fastening it on top of her head with the three hairpins she hadn't lost in the dark.

"Thank you." She reached for Kip's reins.

"You're welcome," Layton murmured. "We'll get down out of these hills, then it's mostly flat prairie from here to Laramie."

She nodded, remembering. "We'll make better time now."

She slid her fingers under the girth. It was a little loose. She didn't want to tighten it with Layton watching, but he didn't move away, so she hooked the stirrup up over the saddle horn and worked at the cinch strap.

"Let me do that." He reached toward her hands.

"It's done." She pulled the knot tight and brought the stirrup down. She didn't want Layton boosting her into the saddle, so she led Kip toward a rock. Holding the reins over his withers, she climbed on the rock and pulled herself into the saddle. She knew Layton was still watching, but she didn't look at him.

Brown was mounting, and Barkley and the buckskin were no

longer in sight. She guessed he was above, watching the trail. She walked Kip toward Brown and the chestnut mare, Lady.

"You all set, Miss Travis?" Brown asked.

"Yes."

He turned Lady toward the trail, and she followed. Barkley and Buck were a darker form against the dark grass and rocks. She could hear Layton's horse behind her.

They headed out without speaking, Barkley leading. Brown followed him, and Amy urged Kip into line behind Lady. They were still moving downward, and they went slowly in the darkness. She wondered how long it would be before the moon would rise. There had been quite a large moon last night, but she didn't know if it was waxing or waning. She tried to remember when it had risen. Before midnight, she thought. She ought to have read that astronomy book of her father's. She felt quite ignorant as she rode on in silence.

There was a steep place in the trail where Barkley dismounted and led his horse down, and they all followed suit. On her westward trip, the corporal guiding her had told her the emigrants unloaded their wagons so the oxen could pull the empty wagons up that slope. Then the travelers carried their belongings up the hill on their backs and reloaded the wagons. She imagined her father carrying the handful of precious books up over the rocky path.

Barkley was waiting at the bottom of the steepest part. Brown led Lady down and moved her out of the way as Kip stepped carefully down. A dark bulk loomed beside the trail.

"What is that?" she asked, and Barkley turned his head to take in the shadowy heap.

"Some of that fine furniture we were talking about."

Behind her, Layton's bay slipped and floundered a little. They all turned quickly.

"Y'all right?" Brown called.

"I think so."

Layton bent and felt the bay's legs carefully.

"That's the worst of it," Barkley said. He swung onto Buck's back, and Amy fumbled for Kip's stirrup before Layton could come and try to help her. They rode slowly for another hour without speaking. The muffled ripple of the river and the even *clop-clop* of the horses' hooves reached her ears. They left the rocky slope, and the hoofbeats were softer on the powder-dry trail.

Barkley pushed Buck into a trot, and they all picked up the pace. After an hour or so, Amy let her mind drift. She was weary, but she had expected that. She felt very alive, and she knew that part of it was the danger, being out here so far from anything with three men she didn't know. They were all polite and sworn to protect her, but still, it kept her senses prickling. The possibility that Indians might appear at any moment made it even more stimulating, though how anything could disturb the quiet darkness of the night, she didn't know. The creak of the leather, the thud of hooves hitting the ground, an occasional snort from one of the horses, the softly murmuring water, and the breeze that whistled past her ears continuously, those were the only sounds as they trotted east on the never-ending trail.

Then Barkley stopped. They all stopped, bunching up behind him.

Amy sat still, listening, trying to divine what had caused his caution. Then she smelled smoke, faint, just a trace. It didn't smell like wood smoke, though: more acrid. Buffalo chips, probably.

Barkley looked around at the three of them.

"Stay here," he said quietly, and the buckskin moved out at a walk. Soon the hoofbeats faded, and Amy shivered. She looked quickly toward Brown. His body was rigid as he strained to hear anything besides the river and the light breeze.

Behind her, Layton's horse snuffled and began cropping grass. Amy wondered if she ought to let Kip grab a mouthful but decided against it. She wanted to hear everything.

For fifteen minutes they sat silently. Kip began to paw, and she stroked his neck soothingly. Far ahead a glow silhouetted the horizon. Again the faint whiff of smoke came to her. Yes, the glow definitely had an orange tinge.

She was about to ask Brown if it were a prairie fire and what they ought to do, when she realized it was the moon, slowly creeping into view. She felt foolish and was glad she hadn't said anything.

Hoofbeats came, a swift staccato. Brown tensed and moved Lady between Amy and the sound.

Before she could take a deep breath and brace herself, she knew that it was Barkley. He reined in next to Lady.

"Seven troopers and a couple of trappers," he said. "They're camping by the river on the way to Bridger. No sign of hostiles since they left Fort Laramie."

"Well, that's good news," said Brown.

Relief swept over Amy. The troopers would more than replace those her father had dispatched as her escort.

Layton moved the bay gelding closer. "So are we going down there to get some hot coffee?"

"No, we're going to keep moving," Barkley said a bit shortly. He turned to Amy. "I asked the corporal to tell your father you'd made it safe this far, Miss Travis."

"Thank you."

"They've got dispatches for him; said the command has changed at Fort Laramie again."

"Major Lynde is gone?" Brown asked.

"Yup. The Fourth Artillery moved in August second with a Colonel John Munroe in charge."

"Are they pulling us out of Bridger?" Layton asked.

"Didn't say. I imagine the dispatches have something to say about your outfit, though." Barkley looked at Amy and smiled. "I reckon we're past the worst danger now, Miss Travis, but we still need to hurry and deliver your father's message to Munroe."

"Of course." She noticed Barkley looked less grave than he had before. "Did you tell them about that wagon train?" she asked.

"Yes, ma'am. They'll watch for it."

"I feel easier knowing they're heading for Bridger," Brown said.

"Me, too." Barkley turned Buck. "Let's go."

They rode on and on, up and down hills and across the prairie, with the undulating grass whispering softly around them. Once they stopped in the darkness to water the horses and let them graze for half an hour. Brown stood watch while the rest of them catnapped.

At sunrise, the view was the same: waving dry grass and the low river that seemed to grow more sluggish as it wound its way east over the plain. But far ahead there were hills and eerie rock formations. Amy pulled her hat brim low as they rode toward the rising sun. She was warmer, so she peeled off her outer shirt, stuffing it into her pack. She knew that within an hour or two the sun's rays would be searing through the thin cotton of her blouse.

Suddenly Brown brought his mare up beside her.

"Indians," he said quietly.

She darted a startled glance at him and looked in the direction he nodded, to the south. She saw three horsemen, perhaps a half mile away, riding over a rise in the prairie, from the southwest.

"Do you think they know we're here?"

"Oh, they saw us."

Amy looked at Barkley's back. "Does he know?"

"He saw them before I did."

Amy shook her head. She must be less observant than she'd thought. But it must be all right or Barkley would have said something.

❧

When the sun was halfway to its apex, Barkley called a halt

once more, and they took the horses cautiously down a faint path to the riverbed. The water level was several feet below the prairie, and they were sheltered from the wind, but Amy felt insecure, as if intruders could approach without warning. She felt a little better when Barkley had released his horse and climbed back up to the prairie above, carrying his rifle.

Brown brought her some food in his neckerchief.

"Thank you. Oh, raisins!" She looked up at him in surprise. "You've been holding out on us."

"I was saving them for the halfway point," he said sheepishly. "A little celebration."

"We're halfway?"

"Ought to see Devil's Gate in an hour and be at Independence Rock within two or three. We're making good time."

Amy found a rock where she could sit at the edge of the placid water and pulled off her boots. Layton and Brown were eating together near the grazing horses. Surreptitiously, she peeled her stockings off and stuffed them in her boots, then dangled her feet in the water. The river was warmer than Sandy Creek had been in the mountains but still refreshingly cool.

She had copied the pioneer women on the trail this summer, for convenience hemming her skirts shorter than was acceptable in the East. Now she arranged her skirt so it was modest without dragging the hem in the water and slowly ate her biscuit and cheese, then chewed the hard, dry raisins one at a time.

Before she had finished, Layton approached.

"You ought to rest while you can, Miss Travis."

She said over her shoulder, "I'm resting. I think this is as good as a nap."

He came closer and squatted at the edge of the water. Amy quickly pulled at her hem, and in the process of trying to cover her ankles, dipped the edge in the water and dropped her last three raisins. Why couldn't the man leave her alone?

"You make a charming picture," he said in a low tone.

She felt her face color. "Please excuse me, Private Layton. I'd like to get up now."

"May I help you?" He held out one hand.

His smile was meant to be engaging, she was sure, but he held no appeal for her. His manner irked her. She didn't want to be flattered.

"No, thank you," she said quickly, perhaps more frostily than was warranted.

"As you wish." He stood and hovered there a moment. "If there's anything I can do, ma'am. . ."

"Thank you. I'm fine."

He went away at last, and she pulled her feet up under her on the rock and stood. The bottom of her riding skirt swished clammily against her legs. She stepped to shore and wiped her feet carefully on the grass, then picked up her boots and stockings and carried them a short way downstream where she could put them on without being stared at. She took out her handkerchief and wet it, wiping a layer of grime from her face.

Brown was lying on a dark brown blanket when she returned, his head on his saddlebags and his hat covering his face. Layton had walked upstream a few paces and chosen a spot where the bank offered a tiny strip of shade. Amy took her blanket and went back to where she had put her boots on. She wanted to take them off again. Her socks were uncomfortably damp, but she didn't want Layton snooping around again when she had bare feet. She lay down on the blanket and shaded her face with her hat.

Its smell reminded her of the day her father had tossed it to her in the sitting room of his quarters. She had been out to ride in the valley with an escort of two privates and come back to the fort flushed and excited. They had seen a bear. Her bonnet was forgotten, hanging down her back by the strings.

"Here," her father had said, flipping the hat into her lap. "If you won't wear a proper bonnet, at least wear this to keep the sun off you. You're turning into a regular hoyden."

But he had smiled, and ever since when she went out to ride, she had worn it along with her boots, a blouse, and a divided skirt, though in the fort she dressed like a proper lady.

Brown woke her when it was time to move on. The sun hung high in the sky, and the heat was oppressive. Kip was saddled and stood waiting for her. Her braid was coming down, and she coiled it and anchored the hairpins more firmly. Before mounting, she drank deeply and wet her handkerchief once more to wipe her face. They met Barkley up on the trail, and she knew he hadn't slept but had let them all rest while he stood watch. She couldn't remember seeing him sleep since they'd left the fort, but he must have, yesterday, while she had slumbered for hours in the shade.

She rode eagerly forward, looking past him to the east, searching the horizon for Devil's Gate, but she couldn't spot the declivity. She trotted Kip up beside the buckskin, hoping Barkley wouldn't find her a nuisance.

He glanced at her, then looked ahead at the trail.

"Think we'll see any more emigrant trains?" she asked.

"It's late. If they haven't made it past Independence Rock by now, they won't get through the Rockies before snowfall."

She looked over at him, then away. The beard stubble was dark on his chin. None of the men had shaved for two days. She hadn't thought about it with Brown, but it made Layton look predatory. On Barkley it was attractive, very masculine.

"Those Indians this morning were Cheyenne," he said.

She was surprised he had brought it up unasked. "Are they friendly?"

"Mostly. They didn't seem to care about us."

She nodded. "So you think we're out of danger?"

"Not out, but getting there." He smiled at her, and her pulse quickened. "Pretty soon you'll be writing a letter to your daddy, telling him you're at Fort Laramie." He looked ahead again and off to the south.

"When?" she asked and wished she hadn't. It sounded childish. But the end of the journey seemed within reach, and she wasn't sure she was glad. She wanted to know that aid was on its way to her father, but she didn't want Barkley to ride off again, leaving her at the fort. She might never see him again.

"Look yonder," he said softly.

She saw it then, the slot in the hills that rose above the plain. "Devil's Gate."

He nodded. "I reckon we can be at the fort in two days. Two long days. And nights." He looked at her again, swiveling slightly in his saddle. "How you holding up?"

"Well, I think."

He nodded, as if he thought so, too. She felt her blush coming on again, but this time she didn't mind. The camaraderie was back, and it was exhilarating. Their horses ran side by side, Kip matching the buckskin's quick trot and reaching over now and again to snap at Buck's jaw.

The wagon trail veered away from the river, but Barkley led them toward the cleft in the rocks. Granite walls rose on either side of them as they entered the pass, and the river rumbled.

"Can't take wagons through here," Barkley yelled.

Amy looked up and saw a slash of blue sky overhead between the cliffs that towered above them. They moved briskly along in the shade until they came out on the east side, and the prairie opened before them once more.

❧

They were nearly within the shadow of Independence Rock, the huge humped stone that rose beside the Sweetwater. Emigrant trains usually stopped there for a rest, but there were no wagons at its base today.

Suddenly Layton cried out behind them, and Barkley turned quickly in the saddle.

Far back on the prairie, three horses were coming fast along the trail from Devil's Gate. Barkley turned Buck around and stood up in his stirrups. Brown and Layton came up to them and faced the west, too.

"Is it those Indians?" Amy asked. Barkley could tell she was frightened, and he wished he could instantly allay her fears.

"No, they're white men." He kept his eyes on the riders, straining for clues to their identity and purpose.

"They're in a big hurry," Brown said. He and Barkley simultaneously pulled their rifles from their scabbards.

"What is it?" Amy asked, her voice shaking slightly.

"Not sure," Barkley said. It didn't feel right. The riders made no signals that would communicate friendship or danger. "Could be they've had some trouble. Get behind me." She wheeled Kip and moved him back. The approaching riders were throwing up alkali dust, but Barkley could see them clearly now, three men riding low over the horses' necks, coming down on them quickly.

"I don't like it," said Brown.

Barkley squinted as his apprehension mounted. "Saw a paint horse like that last night at the troopers' camp."

"You think they ran into some hostiles?" Layton asked, pushing the bay gelding forward a couple of steps.

Barkley shrugged. "We'll know in a minute."

Brown looked hard at him. "We can't go back, T.R."

"I know," Barkley said grimly, keeping his rifle at the ready.

Layton's bay walked forward several more steps. "Those aren't uniforms," he called.

Barkley had already noticed the red shirt on the foremost rider and the buckskins on the next.

"Amy, get in those rocks," he said without turning his head. He heard her horse walking toward the large boulders scattered near the trail. "Could be the trappers that were camping with them last night." He wished they had all taken cover.

As the front horse came within fifty yards of them, he saw the rifle come up.

"Get back!" he yelled, even as smoke billowed.

Layton, several strides ahead of him, jumped as the report cracked, then slumped in the saddle. Brown spurred Lady forward and grabbed the bay's reins as Barkley returned fire. The horseman swerved to his right just as Barkley pulled the trigger. All three riders rode off to the south and circled, just out of range. Brown led Layton's horse quickly toward the rocks, and Barkley crowded Buck behind them.

six

Amy was still astride the big gray, her face chalky. "They shot him," she said incredulously.

Brown dismounted and pulled Layton from the saddle, laying him on the ground in the shelter of the biggest boulder.

"Get down, Amy," Barkley ordered. She was too good a target on the tall gelding. He leaped off Buck's back and found a place where he could watch while reloading, mostly shielded by a boulder. The heat of the rock burned through his shirt as he leaned on it to steady his hands. He poured the powder in from a paper cartridge, followed it with a bullet wrapped in a patch, and rammed it home. He thought he heard a moan from Layton, and he glanced toward Brown as he worked. "How bad, Mike?"

"Real bad. He ain't gonna make it, T.R."

Barkley gritted his teeth, watching the three horses loping toward them again. "They're coming back. Hang on to those horses. We don't want to walk to Fort Laramie."

"I'll hold them." Amy was at his side, pulling Kip along by his bridle.

"You can't hold them all." He relinquished Buck's reins to her and saw that Brown had grabbed Lady's and the bay's.

"Get farther back," he said to Amy. "If they shoot these horses, we won't have much of a chance." Barkley didn't dare watch her as the riders approached again. She came back, panting.

"I hobbled Kip. Let me take the others back there."

Brown let go of the reins, and she ran, pulling Lady and Layton's bay after her.

The three horsemen came relentlessly closer, and Barkley

got another round off before they circled away again. Brown fired as well, but the riders seemed unscathed.

"We need to get out of here." Barkley fumbled to reload. He drew his Colt Dragoon revolver and laid it on the rock in case they rode in too close before he was ready. "We'll tie Layton on his horse. Let them come in one more time, then we head out. Stick to the trail. If they get too close, we'll split up."

"I told you, Layton's had it."

Barkley looked down at the wounded trooper and saw the dark blood soaking the front of his uniform blouse on the left side. He glanced toward the marauders again, and they were far out on the prairie. Bending down, he put his fingers to Layton's neck to feel for a pulse.

"Is he breathing?"

"Don't think so."

Brown frowned, ramming the ball down the barrel of his musket.

Barkley looked out at the riders. They had stopped two hundred yards away and were looking toward them, seemingly in conference. "Check him good," he said through his teeth. "I won't leave him if he's alive, but I won't cut Amy's chances for him if he's dead."

Brown crouched beside his comrade and was silent for several seconds.

He stood up, pointing his rifle toward the three horsemen. "He's dead, T.R."

Barkley swallowed.

"Should we leave his horse?" Brown asked.

"Slow us down if we don't. Take his pistol."

Brown nodded.

"Personal effects?" Barkley asked.

Brown stooped again. Barkley didn't look while he searched the dead trooper's pockets. He stood up again, shoving an envelope into his pocket.

"Letter home," Brown said shortly. He held out Layton's gun belt.

"Where's his rifle?"

"He dropped it."

Barkley looked out to where they had waited on their horses, and he thought he could see a gleam off the gun barrel. He measured the distance from the rock to the gun with his eye. "Best leave it. But we'll take the powder and lead from his pack."

"Here's his knife." Brown held out a sheathed, six-inch blade.

"You take it."

"You don't think we can stand them off?" Brown asked.

"They could keep us pinned down here all day. Don't forget, the major's in need of reinforcements. We've got to get through."

Brown nodded. "You take off with Miss Travis first, and I'll stay here for one more round with those three."

"Oh, no. I'm not leaving you."

"I'll catch up."

Barkley looked at him through narrowed eyes. Somehow, over the last two days, his respect for Brown had deepened into friendship.

"It's the best chance," Brown insisted. "She's the major's daughter. You've got to stick with her. If I keep up the fire, they won't realize you've gone."

Barkley knew that wasn't true. "They'll see the dust." He looked out again toward where Layton's weapon had fallen. "Too bad we can't get his rifle."

"Too risky." Brown rested his musket on the rock, watching the riders.

"Take the horses farther back," Barkley told him. "Turn Layton's horse loose, but drop his tack first. No use giving them a remount."

"After this go-round," Brown agreed.

The attackers were riding in again, low over the necks of

their mounts. Before they were fully in range, Brown fired, and they veered away.

"Save your lead," Barkley told him.

"Sorry. I knew better." Brown began reloading.

"If they'd come a little closer, I could have got that first one," Barkley complained. "I'm pretty sure they're the ones that were with the troopers last night, but I only saw two then. That one with the red shirt, he's a Frenchman."

"What do you think they want?"

"I dunno. They said last night they were heading up the Sweetwater, scouting for beaver."

"I'm guessing they think we've got something important, like an army payroll or something." Brown poured powder down the barrel of his gun.

"Heading east? That makes no sense."

"Well, the only thing we've got that's worth anything is Miss Travis."

Barkley stared at him.

"Did you tell them last night?" Brown asked gently.

"I told the corporal, but I didn't make a general announcement. Someone might have heard, I guess, or he might have told them after I left." He felt sick, realizing he might have caused the attack, Layton's death, and Amy's immediate peril. He reached for Brown's rifle. "Go fix the horses."

Brown slipped between the rocks, and Barkley kept his eyes on the three riders, who stopped once more on the prairie, then faced him again.

"God, help us get her out of here," he whispered fervently, leaning Brown's gun, muzzle up, against the rock and hefting his own rifle to draw a bead on the lead rider's shirt.

He waited until they rode in close. Their bullets ricocheted wildly off the stones, one throwing up chips of granite in his face. He held steady and pulled the trigger.

Brown was back, breathing hard, shoving a bag of ammunition into his hand. "All set. Leave Lady ground tied for me."

"What if she follows us?"

Brown didn't have an answer.

"I'd better bring her up here," Barkley said.

"This is taking too long."

"I know. I think I winged one of them."

He reloaded, seized his six-shooter, and left Brown, dodging through the boulders to where Amy was waiting with Buck and Kip. Layton's horse was free, already moving eastward, snatching grass as he trotted away from the noise. The saddle and bridle lay in a heap, and Lady stood off to one side, content for now to stand patiently, waiting for Brown.

"I'm taking her up there for him." Barkley took hold of Lady's reins.

"Private Brown said we're leaving him behind." Her eyes were huge.

"He'll catch up."

A look of pain crossed her face, and he felt guilty. It had been his own reaction to the plan, but she thought it was his idea.

He took Lady up to a rock just behind the trooper.

"What are they doing?" he called.

"Getting ready for another pass."

"Think they'd talk?"

"What do you think?" Brown replied.

Barkley anchored Lady's reins with a small rock.

"Keep to the south bank, and I'll try to lead them off," Brown yelled.

Barkley hesitated.

"Get going!"

"I'll see you later!" It was a hope rather than a promise.

ૹ

Amy struggled to breathe calmly as Barkley ran back toward her. It seemed all wrong to be leaving Private Brown, but she couldn't stop trusting the scout's judgment now.

"Let's go!"

She turned toward Kip and reached for the stirrup, but

Barkley came behind her and picked her up bodily, swinging her atop the horse. Startled, she gathered up the reins. He was on Buck, giving a last backward look as shots rang out again.

"Stick with me!" he ordered, and the buckskin pounded down the trail, eastward, away from the shooting.

She let Kip run flat out for the first time. He tore up the ground, and soon his nose was only inches from Buck's flying black tail. They rode on and on, and she looked back once but could not see any movement, could not even see the boulders anymore, just Independence Rock rising calm and solid over the waving grasses.

Barkley slowed his horse. The Sweetwater had tumbled into the Platte, and they had reached one of several points where the wagon trail crossed the river. It was shallow and muddy. In the spring it had been a torrent, and it had been rafted across.

Barkley looked back. "We'll stick to the south bank. Maybe they'll think we followed the trail and went across."

"Can't we wait for Brown?" she asked.

He pressed his lips together and urged Buck into a gallop again.

She thought she heard a shot and looked behind her. Far back, she saw a reddish horse charging up the riverbank.

"It's Brown!" she screamed, and she raised her arm, waving wildly.

Barkley stopped and wheeled Buck around. "Get down!"

"What?"

He rode close to her and pulled her out of the saddle, even as he slid from Buck's back.

"But Brown won't—" She stopped. Brown was splashing into the water at the ford, and now she could see the three horses behind him.

The buckskin was lying down in the tall grass. Amy couldn't believe it. She turned to stare at Barkley and saw that he was pulling Kip's head down until the gray lay down, too. Then she understood.

"They'll kill Private Brown," she choked.

"I hope not."

He grasped her upper arm and pulled her down, then crouched beside her, listening. They heard a distant shout, and she could hear the hoofbeats clearly. Her heart pounded. She hoped they wouldn't come to where they hid, but she didn't want them to catch Brown, either.

Barkley half stood, peering intently toward the ford. "Get up. Quick."

He tugged at the reins, and both horses clambered to their feet. Again he picked her up and tossed her into the saddle. She didn't have time to think about how strong he was. She only had time to get her boots into the stirrups and hang on as Kip took off at a dead run after the buckskin. They veered out away from the riverbank and rode for five miles, parallel to the Platte. She looked across the wide riverbed often but couldn't see the mysterious riders or Brown. The ground was rough in places, and they crossed a stream that meandered toward the river. Kip was breathing hard but not gasping. She could see that Buck's sides were heaving.

❧

Barkley led her on at a frantic pace. He regretted pushing Buck so hard, but Amy's peril overshadowed everything else. At last they approached a place where four large cottonwoods grew beside the river, and he headed for them. When they were beneath the trees, he stopped and leaped to the ground.

"Don't unsaddle. We'll let them breathe and cool down a little, then give them a drink. Then we go on."

"Are we safe now?" she asked timidly as she dismounted.

"No."

"They followed Brown."

He turned away from her accusing eyes, leading Buck slowly in a circle beneath the trees. "It was the only way. Brown has as good a chance as any man under the circumstances."

"Even you?"

Barkley frowned. He ought to be the one drawing off the outlaws, not Mike Brown. Mike had a family. But he had promised the major he would stay with Amy no matter what. He personally would deliver her to Fort Laramie. He gritted his teeth.

"I've already caused the death of one loyal man," she said. Tears stood in her eyes.

"It's not your fault, Amy."

"You can say that, but if I weren't along, Layton and Brown would be back at Fort Bridger."

"Yes, and fighting Indians hand to hand, no doubt," he flung at her. He stopped and sighed, putting one foot up on a rock, gazing across the river, and praying silently for Brown.

When he turned to look at her, she was holding Kip's reins loosely, letting him crop the dry grass. Her eyes were hard; her face troubled.

"Come on, let's water them," he said. "We need to move."

"Brown is mustering out in January." She blinked hard against the tears.

"I know." He took the reins from her hand and led both horses to the water. He wished they could stop longer and rest them. Buck had heart, but he couldn't run forever.

Amy followed him to the edge of the water. "If Brown escapes—" she began, then stopped.

"It's not Brown they're after."

"What, then?"

He said nothing.

"It's me," she said flatly. "You think they want me."

"It's all I can figure," he admitted. "They might be hoping to get a ransom."

"A ransom?" she snorted. "Army majors don't make much."

He was silent. He knew that when they discovered Brown had decoyed them away from her, they would come back.

Buck lifted his head, and Barkley said, "Let's move."

They rode on in bleak silence, cantering the horses. Whenever Barkley looked at Amy, she was looking somewhere else, her face a mask of grief. His heart twisted. Even if he managed to fulfill her father's commission, he had failed her.

seven

The sun was dropping behind them when Barkley slowed again. Amy thought of how happy she'd felt that morning, when he'd told her they would be at Fort Laramie in two days. Now she wondered if they would reach the fort at all. He was calling her Amy now. That would have thrilled her a few hours ago, but now it was simply an expedient. He could bark orders at her faster if he didn't say *Miss Travis*.

She was so tired, she hardly noticed when Kip stopped. Barkley was standing beside her horse in the dusk, touching her elbow.

"Come on down. We need to rest." She slid off to the side, and he caught her and stood her upright. "You get some sleep. I'll keep a lookout."

They were near the river again, but the bank came right up to the prairie grass. Barkley spread a blanket in the short, curly buffalo grass for her.

"Try to sleep." He pushed her gently toward the blanket.

"It's my fault," she mumbled.

"No. Don't think that." He gripped her arm. "Look at me, Amy."

She turned and looked up into his face, and she couldn't hate him. The sorrow in his eyes was so deep, she knew he was as grieved as she.

"Brown came up with this plan. He wanted to do it this way. He knew I couldn't leave you, and it seemed like the best chance."

Her mind was whirling, and she focused on his brown eyes. He looked wounded.

"Amy, it's not your fault. It's mine. I told that corporal we were taking you to Laramie. I shouldn't have told anyone you were with us. If I'd realized—" He turned away sharply and seized the horses' reins, heading for the river.

"Mr. Barkley," she called.

He dropped the leather straps and walked back to her slowly. Kip and Buck lowered their heads and began grazing. He stood before her, his shoulders slouched, his eyes pleading.

"I'm sorry," he whispered. "It wasn't supposed to be like this."

She nodded and swallowed hard. She felt she knew him very well now, had seen him at his best in the display of staunch courage at Independence Rock. And now she was witness to his worst, the guilt and the agonizing regret.

"Do you have a name besides Barkley?" Her voice was hoarse from the tears she hadn't shed.

His lips twitched. "Folks call me T.R."

"What does it stand for?"

He looked toward the horses, then back. "Thomas Randolph."

"Thomas. May I call you that? Mr. Barkley seems a bit formal now."

He licked his chapped lips and looked past her. She wondered if he was uncomfortable with her request and was trying to think of a way to politely say no.

"Tom," he said at last.

She nodded. "All right, Tom. If I'm going to stop blaming myself, you have to, too. We have to concentrate on surviving and getting to Fort Laramie as fast as we can, agreed?"

He reached out tentatively and put his hand on her shoulder for an instant, then backed away. She watched him lead the horses down to the river, then she lay down on the blanket. The evening star shone brightly near the horizon in the west. There was no one to spell Tom Barkley on the lookout. Before she could think about that, her mind had shut down and she slept, dreamless.

ॐ

He let her sleep for an hour and wished it could be longer. She was bone tired, he knew, but if they lingered here, the riders might catch up. He paced along the riverbank. If he weren't so sleepy, he could think more clearly. His plan had exploded in chaos, and his misery weighed him down. But he knew that somehow this all had to be part of God's plan, whether they survived or not. He couldn't lose sight of that. It was up to him to keep Amy moving toward Fort Laramie. Only that much was in his control.

It was nearly dark. Time to move.

He looked into her innocent face before he woke her, wishing she could awaken to a world where everything was good and true and right. He put two fingers out and touched her smooth cheek.

"Amy." It was barely a whisper. He cleared his throat and tried again. "Amy, wake up."

Her eyelashes fluttered, and she looked up into his face. He caught his breath, and slowly she smiled, just a small smile that might mean recognition or friendship, but it reassured him. She wasn't angry. She was sad, but she didn't despise him for leading the two troopers to death or for revealing her presence to the trappers.

"God knows, Tom," she said softly.

"Yes, I reckon He does. We have to trust Him."

He took her hand and pulled her to her feet, then picked up the blanket.

He had brought food from the saddlebag, and she ate her share as they walked to the horses. He hadn't dared to unsaddle in case the riders appeared while she slept.

Amy lifted the stirrup and checked Kip's girth. "What's this?" She was staring at the belt tied to her bedroll.

"It's Layton's pistol. In case we get separated." He heard her take a deep breath. "Can you shoot?"

"A little."

"It's a six-shot, but you have to load each chamber. They're all loaded now."

"I don't think I could reload it." She looked up at him apologetically.

"Well, we'll hope you don't need to."

"Think Buck is rested?"

"Yes, he'll be all right for a while." He'd be glad when they reached the fort and he could turn the faithful buckskin out for a few days.

She was in the saddle before he could offer to help, and he reflected that it was just as well. Feelings for her had taken root in his heart, but his mission was to get her to a place where she could ride out of his life forever.

He mounted, glancing across at her before signaling Buck to move out. Suddenly he stiffened. He heard hoofbeats, distant but coming toward them from the west.

She heard them, too; he could see that. She was afraid, but she sat still, looking to him for direction.

"Ride, Amy. Stick to the riverbank. Keep going no matter what happens! The wagon road crosses the Platte again about ten miles from here, and you can pick it up on this side. Go!"

"I'm not leaving you." It was a sob.

"I'll be right behind you. You go first, and be careful, but don't spare the horse. Now move!" He yanked his rifle from the scabbard.

≈

She headed Kip eastward and tore off, looking back over her shoulder to be sure Tom followed. Buck was running, head down in the twilight.

She turned forward, trying to watch the trail ahead for obstacles. Kip ran so fast that she couldn't focus on objects before they were past. The faint track was barely distinguishable in the growing darkness. She would have to trust Kip, at least until moonrise. She knew now that the moon was waning. It would rise later and be smaller than last night. Clouds had moved in while she slept. Perhaps there would be no moonlight at all.

She looked behind her and saw that Kip was rapidly outdistancing Buck. She knew Tom would have only one shot with his musket. She prayed their pursuers would not come within pistol range.

"Dear God, help us!" Her words were snatched away by the wind. She felt her braid flopping against her shoulders. The last of the hairpins had loosened. She clapped one hand hard on her hat, pulling the band down tight above her ears.

She pulled Kip down to a canter, hating to disobey Tom but unwilling to lose sight of him. Buck was a quarter mile back, and she could barely see him. She held the gray at the slower pace until half the distance was closed, then she kept him moving steadily on. She wasn't sure how long Buck could keep running, but she knew she wasn't going to desert Tom.

Half an hour later, she couldn't stand it. It was very dark. She stopped Kip and sat listening. The gelding gave a cough and breathed heavily, but she could hear hoofbeats behind her. She couldn't see Buck. What if it wasn't him? What if the strange men swooped down on her out of the darkness? She looked around hopelessly for cover, but there was none.

The buckskin came cantering out of nothing, suddenly appearing a few yards away.

"Tom!"

He checked his horse.

"Amy! I told you to go!"

"I did, but—"

"Keep going!"

She swung Kip into step beside him, and the two horses picked up the long trot they used for travel.

"Are they coming?" she asked.

"Yes, but their horses are tired, too."

"Do you think Brown got away?" she dared to say.

"I don't know. But now they know where we are."

To the north, lightning flashed, and a few seconds later, a deep thunderclap rumbled over the prairie.

"We're in for it," Tom said.

Amy thought the prospect of rain was delicious. She felt so parched. Her lips were dry and scaly, and her hands felt leathery from their constant exposure to wind and sun.

"Ford's up ahead," he said. The wagon road would be plain after that, but its ruts might trip up the horses. "Let's hope these clouds blow over and we get some moonlight."

When they came to the place where the trail came up out of the Platte, he led her to the water. They stayed in the saddle as the horses stretched their necks down to drink greedily. Tom was listening, watching back to the west.

"How far behind are they?" she breathed.

"Not far. Here, fill the canteens, and I'll hold Kip's reins."

She slipped from the saddle, waded a few steps upstream from the animals, and stooped to fill the two canteens. She sloshed back to Kip and handed them to Tom, and he fastened them to the saddles as she mounted.

"Let's go," he said, and she pulled Kip's head up.

Tom kept Buck at a trot, and she and Kip stayed beside them. The two horses kept to the wagon ruts, with a slight ridge of dry grass between them. The river wound away from them, and they continued more or less straight for a couple of miles. The lightning flashed intermittently.

"This storm could work to our advantage," Tom said.

"Think so?"

"Well, we'll probably get soaked, but it might make them hole up somewhere."

"The horses can't keep on forever." It was really Buck she was worried about. Even Kip was tired; she could tell by his dragging steps and his drooping neck. Buck must be near exhaustion.

Tom was silent a moment, then said, "I don't dare to stop now. They weren't far behind me back there. I can't hear them now, but they know we're here. They might stop to rest for a while and figure they can catch up to us in the morning. We'll just keep going slow for now, all right?"

He was asking her opinion. She wasn't sure she liked that. All her life, she'd depended on strong men to order her life— first her father; her brother-in-law while she lived in his home; then her father again; and now Tom Barkley. She wanted him to give orders again, to be confident, and to know what was best. But then, she wanted Brown and Layton back, too, and she wanted to be safe at Fort Laramie, not out here in the dark wilderness with three evil men pursuing her. She took a deep, shaky breath.

"Whatever you think, Tom."

&

The rain held off, although the thunder rumbled louder. Tom looked frequently over his shoulder, but the flashes of lightning revealed no one on the back trail. At last they came back to the verge of the Platte, at a place where large cottonwoods clung to the bank. They took the horses down for a drink beneath the trees, and this time they dismounted.

"Let's let them graze for a few minutes," he said. "Keep hold of Kip's bridle, though."

He unstrapped Layton's gun belt and put it in her saddlebag. She wouldn't be able to use it effectively as she rode. Better to keep it dry. They stood next to each other, and the horses began pulling grass, tugging against the taut reins. Tom stretched his arms and legs. He listened as he prayed continuously.

He wondered if Amy was praying. She was his sole reason for living now. She might be his reason for dying. She had mentioned God, and he wanted to know how deep her faith was and where she looked for solace in her worst moment.

"Amy?"

"What?"

"Do you. . .pray?"

"Yes."

"Are you praying now?"

"Yes."

He reached out, and his hand found hers. "Me, too."

She squeezed his fingers, and his heart jumped.

"He won't leave us, Amy. No matter what happens."

She was silent a moment, clinging to his hand. "Thank you."

He listened once more, but the river swirled and the wind moaned. The intermittent thunder blasts dulled his hearing. They couldn't stay here. They wouldn't hear anyone approaching. At least the horses had gotten a drink and a few mouthfuls of grass.

"Let's go."

They fumbled wearily with the reins in the darkness. Amy was in the saddle before Tom could reach her side to help her. The thunder crashed, and Kip squealed and sidestepped.

Tom yelled, "We'd better get away from these trees."

She got the gray under control and followed him away from the water. They picked up the trail at a trot once more.

The horses were fidgety. When Amy stroked Kip's neck, a spark crackled from her hand. The gray snorted and pulled against the bit.

"He wants to run."

"Too dangerous," Tom said.

The wind was suddenly much stronger, and rain began to fall in big, splattering globs. The horses snuffled and twitched, but still they trotted onward. The drops pelted them, soaking their clothing. They puddled on Tom's hat and funneled off the brim, down the back of his shirt.

At first it felt good to be wet and cool all over, but soon his wet clothing started to chafe his skin. The wind stole his body heat, and he began to shiver. It was worse for Amy, he knew. She wasn't used to being out in all kinds of weather, the way he was. He had to find shelter.

The lightning struck close, hitting a tree near the river, and

Kip reared with a terrified squeal as a deafening crash of thunder broke over them.

"Amy!"

She fought the gelding's panic, speaking quietly and holding his head down firmly. "Ho, Kip, easy."

Tom pushed Buck up beside them, reaching toward Kip's bridle. He seized the reins just below Kip's bit and added his strength to Amy's. "You all right?"

"Yes," she yelled, "but I don't know how long I can hold him."

"Stick close to me!"

≈

They rode along slowly, so close their stirrups brushed, and Tom kept one hand on Kip's bridle. He watched the trail sharply and looked frequently off to the right. Amy was sure he was searching for something.

She leaned toward him. "What are you looking for?"

"An old man used to have a cabin off here someplace. I haven't been there in three or four years, but I think I can find it."

They kept the horses at a walk. Kip fretted against the bit, trying to get his head down. Amy hated not being able to trust the magnificent horse, but she didn't dare test his loyalty to her. Under ordinary circumstances, she would have been livid if a man implied that she couldn't handle a horse. But Kip was far stronger than she was, and in his present frenzy, she was afraid he would bolt given the smallest opportunity, so she swallowed her pride and allowed Tom to hold on.

Both horses began to slip in the mud that was forming in the wagon ruts. Every time the thunder boomed, Buck shuddered, but he kept on steadily. Kip lunged and pawed at each crash. In a flicker of lightning, Amy saw the gray's head twisted back toward her. The whites of his eyes showed starkly, and foam dripped from his bit as he threw his head from side to side in terror.

eight

Vainly, Tom looked for a place where they could take shelter. They kept moving in the drenching downpour, and at last he was rewarded by the dark hulk of hills rising on their right. The trail skirted the northern end of the range where it came close to the Platte, and he knew they were near his goal. He thought he saw a faint track leaving the wagon road, and he stopped Buck, calling to Amy to try to hold Kip steady. A bright flicker of lightning came, and Kip jerked against his weight. But in that light, Tom recognized the place.

"This way!" He waited until Kip stopped prancing, then released the reins. He turned Buck in at the overgrown path. Most travelers went right past it, never suspecting there was a dwelling nearby. Trusting the rain to obliterate their tracks, Tom urged Buck up the trail and around a knoll, and there it was: an adobe cabin built twenty years or more ago by old Jim Frye. The codger had been dead several years, and an Irish family had squatted in the cabin one winter, but as far as Tom knew, it was deserted now.

There was no light, no smoke. He rode up and dismounted.

He stood in the doorway until lightning came again, showing him the place was empty. A corner of the roof was missing, and water poured in on that side of the ten-by-fifteen-foot cabin. He led Buck over the threshold and pulled him to one side, then went out again.

"Get down," he shouted up at Amy.

Slowly, she brought her right leg over Kip's back and hung there for a moment, her left foot still in the stirrup. He reached up and put his hands on her waist.

"Jump, Amy."

She kicked the stirrup off and plopped down beside him. He shoved her toward the door and pulled Kip by the reins, one hand on his nose, trying to lower the big animal's head so he could get through the doorway. The horse balked for an instant, sniffing, then plunged through the gap.

Tom shut the door.

"Amy?"

"Here."

He jumped, she was so close in the darkness.

"The roof is leaking over there," he said.

"I h–hear it."

"I think I saw a bunk to the left."

Her hand clutched his wrist. She was shaking.

"You're freezing!" he said. The lightning blazed, and he saw that there was no mattress or bedding, just a plain wooden bunk against the wall.

He led Amy to it. "Sit down," he said in her ear. "I'll get your blanket."

He spoke quietly to the horses, groping in the darkness. They moved restlessly in the small space, snorting and snuffling. Buck stood still for him, and he worked the soggy leather strap until he was able to lift the saddle off, then stripped the bridle off, too, feeling for a place to lay them against the wall. His bedroll felt wet, and he left it on the saddle. Guided by flashes of lightning, he went to Kip and unsaddled him. He fumbled with the rawhide thongs that kept Amy's blanket against the cantle. The smell of wet wool and leather filled his nostrils. At last he got the blanket free and stumbled toward the bunk with it.

"Here, the inside isn't too bad," he said, but he knew the whole thing was too wet to do her much good. They needed a fire.

He had gathered by now that there was a small cast-iron stove in the room, but he couldn't see anything they could burn. He felt the saddle blankets, but they were soaked with rain and sweat.

"You all right?" he asked.

"I think so."

"I wish we could have a fire."

"They'd smell the smoke," she said.

"That's if we had anything to burn."

She chuckled. He was glad she could laugh. It meant the storm hadn't drained as much of her energy as he'd feared. He was freezing but couldn't take off his wet clothes.

"If Buck wasn't sopping wet, we could make him lie down and let him keep us warm," she said in the blackness.

It startled him that she was thinking in the same direction he was.

"There aren't any blankets here?" she asked.

"I haven't seen anything. Just the bunk and the stove. Indians probably pilfered everything else."

※

Amy tried to concentrate on a different part of the cabin each time the lightning flashed, until she had looked at every inch of it. The horses took up most of the space on the packed earth floor. There were no cupboards or boxes, no pans or clothing. Nothing. At least it had a roof. Sort of.

"Sit down, Tom." She realized he was standing beside the bunk, looking around in the irregular bursts of light the way she was. But the last time, she thought he'd been looking at her.

"I'm dripping wet."

"So am I."

"Hold on."

She heard him working at something and, when the lightning came, saw that he had opened his saddlebag and found his flannel shirt. It was surely the only dry piece of cloth in the cabin except maybe the dirty socks and blouse in her own pack.

Still the rain drummed down in torrents. At least there were no leaks over the bunk. Amy sat upright, shivering on the hard wood, her legs curled under her.

She felt the bunk give a little as he sat down on the edge

and thrust the soft shirt into her hands.

"Here, put this on."

"Your extra shirt?"

"Yes."

"You should wear it."

"No, I'm all right. Put it on."

Meekly, she slipped her arms into the sleeves. She felt marginally warmer and raised her wrist to her face, inhaling the comforting fragrance of Tom's shirt.

He got up and went back to the pile of gear, returning with her saddlebags.

"The gun's in this one," he said, guiding her hand to the buckle. "Keep it on the bunk beside you."

He went to the slot that was more of a rifle loop than a window and looked out. She was less uncomfortable but still shivering. Her skirt hung in heavy, wet folds.

"Do you think they're out there?" she called over the noise of the rain.

"I don't know."

"If they know about this place, they may come here."

"I thought of that, but we had to take a chance." He came back to the bunk and sat down beside her.

She had to admit that being inside the cabin was a lot better than being out on the trail. "You're right, Tom. We'll have to pray they don't know about it."

The wind howled around the little house. If it didn't tear off the rest of the roof, they'd be fairly secure.

"Can you sleep?" he asked.

"I don't think so." She wrapped her arms around herself, tucking her hands under her arms. She was so cold! She clamped her teeth together to keep them from chattering.

"Here." He pulled the damp blanket up over her shoulders. She wasn't sure the wet wool army blanket would help, but she accepted it. He shifted beside her, and she leaned back, sitting against the cabin wall.

"What'll we do if they come?" she asked.

"Well, we've got the rifle and two pistols. These walls will stop bullets, I think. But if they start shooting at the door and windows. . ."

She looked toward the two narrow slots of windows. There didn't seem to be any shutters.

"If they come and start shooting in here, get behind the stove," Tom said. "Keep the pistol with you. And if I go down—"

"Don't say that!"

He sighed. "Amy, listen. It could happen. I don't think it will. I think they're huddled under some rock right now, waiting this storm out, but if it does happen, you've got to be ready."

She took a long, ragged breath, pushing down the fear. "All right. What do I do?"

He spoke slowly and deliberately, and his voice was the only reality for her in the darkness. "If I go down, use those six shots well. Don't shoot wildly. Wait until they're close. I think the powder's dry. If the pistol misfires, stay calm and try again."

"All right. But you'll be here."

&

Tom wasn't sure how to deal with her blind faith in him. Did she think he was invincible? He'd already shown his weakness. He had revealed the existence of his precious cargo to crafty adversaries. He ought to have just told the corporal to tell Major Travis he had met him and that all was well. Once again, he fought guilt and depression. He had to think about this minute and how to keep her safe.

"Funny, we were worrying about Indians all that time." She sounded hoarse, and she had to yell for him to hear over the pounding rain and the wind.

"Those trappers," he said, leaning toward her. "I can't figure it out. I never expected this."

"What are they like?" she asked.

"I only saw two of them by firelight. One's a Frenchman, dark, with a bushy beard. One's a big man that seemed to talk a lot. The third one. . .well, he was wearing buckskins when they attacked us. He might have been in the camp when I was there, but I didn't see him."

She sat thoughtfully for a few minutes, and Tom closed his eyes, trying to picture the men he had glimpsed so briefly.

"The Frenchman," she said, leaning close to his ear. "How did you know he was French?"

"He spoke to me at the troopers' camp. Name's LeBeau or LaBelle or something like that."

She caught her breath. "There was a man named LeBeau at Fort Bridger."

"When?"

"He came in June, I think. Father had him in custody when we left."

"Why?"

"He'd been gambling with the men. There was a fight one night, I think, and they told him to leave and. . ." She hesitated, and Tom wondered how much her protective father had told her. "I think he tried to steal one of the troopers' horses."

"So the major had him locked up?"

"Yes, for several weeks before we left."

"Had he seen you before that?"

"Yes, several times. But it couldn't be the same man."

"I don't see how, either."

"Father was waiting for orders, I think. He had sent word to Fort Laramie about it and was waiting for someone to tell him what to do."

"Maybe they'll hang him," Tom said. "Or if the Indians attack the fort, they might let him go if he promises to fight." He couldn't see what it had to do with the attack at Independence Rock. The men pursuing them had come out of the east with the troopers. He was certain now they had left the troopers and followed them back. There had to be a reason.

"Is your father independently wealthy?" he asked.

In the flickering light, he saw her wide eyes staring toward him. "No, I told you. Are you still thinking they want a ransom?"

"You never know. If the rumor got around that your family was rich. . ."

"Other than his pay, he has nothing."

"Hm."

He settled back against the adobe wall, and Amy leaned back, too. Her shoulder touched his, and he wondered if he should pull away, but she was so warm, he didn't. She pulled the damp blanket around in front of her.

"Here, take part of this, Tom. The bottom end is soaked, but the top part is merely saturated."

He laughed and pulled the scratchy blanket over his legs and up around his chest. "You're exaggerating. This part's hardly dripping."

She chuckled, and he settled back, letting his arm rest against hers. Her heat reached him through their sleeves. The lightning came less often, and he couldn't see her, but he imagined she had her feet curled under her on the bunk again, beneath the blanket.

"Still cold?" he asked.

"Not so bad. What time do you think it is?"

"I don't know. After midnight. Try to sleep if you can." He realized he was talking in a normal voice and she was hearing him. The thunderclaps came less frequently, and the rain had softened from the violent deluge to a steady downpour. "Maybe the storm's blowing over," he hazarded.

"Should we leave?"

"Not yet. But it does seem to be letting up."

She sat not moving. A bolt of lightning flickered, and he saw that she was leaning her head back against the wall, her eyes closed. She looked utterly peaceful, and he wanted to keep her that way. He wished he could block the door somehow in case the marauders came. His fatigue was catching up with him, and he closed his eyes, wondering hazily if he could make Buck lie down in front of the door. There had to be something.

"Maybe we could drag the stove over in front of the door," she said suddenly. "It's not doing us any good where it is."

Tom sat up. "That's uncanny. I was just thinking about it."

She laughed. "If we're both thinking it, we'd best do it."

"Well, it's not big enough to keep them out, but it would slow them down."

"I'll help."

The lightning flashed again. Tom pulled the stovepipe loose, and they hefted the box stove toward the door, crowding the horses aside as they went. It was heavier than he'd expected, and he was glad Amy was bearing a portion of the weight. When it was settled in front of the door, he felt the tiniest bit easier. He looked long out the window loops, but everything appeared the same.

The river will be rising, he thought. There were still a couple of places where the road crossed the Platte. It might be dangerous to ford now. The horses would have to swim.

When he turned back to the bunk, he thought Amy was asleep, her back against the wall. She had removed her boots and pulled her feet up beneath her skirt, but she lifted the edge of the blanket as he sat down, so he settled in next to her. It was hard to get comfortable without feeling too self-conscious, so near to a woman. He sat still and listened to the rain, the heavy breathing of the horses, and Amy's softer breath, close to his ear now.

Why had he stayed out of her path at Fort Bridger? he wondered. She embodied everything in his nebulous idea of the perfect woman. If he'd met her a few months ago. . .but no, he hadn't been ready then, and Benjamin Travis wouldn't have accepted him as a suitor for Amy. Some captain, maybe, or even a first lieutenant, but not a scout. Now if he got her to safety, she was heading into that other world. He doubted their paths would ever cross again. She might insist on waiting at Fort Laramie to hear the outcome of the Indian uprising, but she wouldn't stay there long.

He was nearly asleep when her head settled, very gently, on his shoulder, jolting him awake. His pulse raced. Her breath was even, and he was sure she was sleeping. The major's daughter wouldn't lean on a scout if she were conscious. He didn't move, not wanting to disturb her. She needed to rest, and he didn't want to embarrass her.

All right, he admitted to himself, *I like this.* Maybe it was time to think seriously about finding a wife. Immediately he rejected the idea. He didn't want to go looking. Amy was everything he wanted, but she was far beyond his reach. And any other female he encountered would be measured unfavorably against her.

nine

When Tom awoke, Buck was nudging his boot as he snuffled around the dirt floor, no doubt looking for something edible. Beyond him, Kip stood, knees locked, sleeping. Dawn was fast approaching.

He turned his head toward the window, realizing all at once that his left arm encircled Amy's shoulders, holding her against his side, and her head was pillowed just below his collar bone. And he was wonderfully warm.

He sat still, breathing carefully, not sure what to do. How had this happened?

The rain seemed to have faded to a light drizzle. He ought to get up and look out the windows and begin to get the horses ready. Carefully, he shifted, easing his arm up a bit. Her head stirred, and she nestled in closer. He held his breath. Her left hand was sliding across the front of his shirt, toward his right shoulder.

This is not good, he told himself. *We'll both be embarrassed when she wakes up. She'll hate me.*

He lowered his head and just for a second let his cheek rest against her hair. Then very carefully, he inched away from her, sliding his arm off her and moving toward the edge of the bunk.

He thought he could settle her on the wooden platform, but as her head gently came down on her arm, her eyelids flew open and she sat up quickly, blinking at him with those huge blue eyes. One hand went to her disheveled braid, where loose hairs danced around her ears and neck. The other pulled the wool blanket around her.

"Is it time?" she asked, her voice husky from sleep.

82

"I think so. Just stay there, and I'll take a look outside."

❧

He walked to the nearest window, and Amy sat on the bunk watching him. Her heart was pounding. Tom stood immobile for a full minute, and something made her sit still, watching him. His hair was tousled, and the tails of his soft shirt hung down. He looked like a little boy who needed some mothering. She smiled at that assessment, compared with her first impressions of him at Fort Bridger. He was tough, independent, a loner who would get the job done with no fuss. No one would stand in his way. That was why her father had picked him, wasn't it?

"I'm going to look around outside," he said, putting his hat on. "It's still raining but not hard. If there's no sign of them, I think we ought to go on."

She nodded. "I'll gather things up."

Tom dragged the stove to one side, then cautiously opened the door and stood looking down the path that led to the wagon trail and the river. With his rifle in hand, he stepped out and closed the door. A cool draft stole through the room, and Amy realized the heat of the animals had raised the temperature inside the cabin during the night. She didn't relish riding on in the rain and getting soaked again, but there seemed no alternative. They couldn't afford to delay.

She combed her hair out and tied it back with a bit of blue ribbon from her saddlebag. She shook out Kip's saddle blanket and spoke softly to him as she stood on tiptoe to spread it over his back. By the time Tom returned, she had saddled both horses and was fastening her damp bedroll with the leather thongs on Kip's saddle.

"I checked the road. No fresh tracks," Tom said. "We'd better get going."

"The biscuits are getting stale," she said without looking up. "I thought we ought to eat them now."

She nodded toward the bunk, where she had set out four

biscuits. Tom walked over and picked one up.

He bit into it and grimaced. "You didn't make these, did you?"

She chuckled and tied the last knot in the rawhide thong. "No, those are army-issue biscuits. I wouldn't claim them."

"That's a relief."

She sneaked a look at him, and his humor changed quickly to dismay. "Your lip is bleeding."

She put one finger to her lower lip, then looked at the trace of blood on it. "Every time you make me laugh, the skin cracks and bleeds."

"Sorry."

"Don't be. Laughing is good." She picked up Kip's bridle. She could see that Tom's lips were chapped, too. "Wish we had some lard."

"Lard? Guess that would help. Wouldn't taste bad on these biscuits, either."

She laughed, then winced. "You're doing it again."

"Sorry." He swallowed the last of the biscuit and shook his canteen before opening it for a small sip. "We ought to be at Fort Laramie by tomorrow morning."

"Really?" She felt he was holding it out to her as consolation for all the discomfort she was enduring. She tried not to stare into his intent brown eyes. If she did that, she might give away too much of the confusion that was swirling in her heart. *It's because you have to depend on him right now,* she told herself. *This is not love. It's admiration and respect and tension brought on by danger.*

Tom reached for Buck's bridle. "It's about a hundred miles from here. We can do it in a day if everything goes right. We'll have to rest a few times, but I think we can make it."

His confidence renewed her determination. With that little bit of encouragement from him, she was ready to face another grueling day. They would survive, and her father would be proud of her.

Tom went out first, the musket at the ready. Amy waited,

looking over his shoulder, as he stood silent for half a minute, listening. It was nearly full daylight, and the rain pattered down on the trees surrounding the cabin. Faintly, she heard the roar of the river.

He turned and took Buck's reins from Amy's hand. She moved Kip aside, and the buckskin plunged through the doorway into the light with a glad little snuffle.

"They're hungry," Amy said as she led Kip out.

"I know, but we'd better get away from here before we let them graze. We need to get to a place where we can see the trail for a ways."

She mounted quickly, and they walked the horses down the trail, coming out on the wagon road sooner than she had expected.

"What a mess." She looked dolefully at the wet wagon ruts.

"Stay in the middle," Tom said. "You go first. I'll be right behind you. Just keep heading east."

She set out with Kip, and the sun came up, chasing the last of the rain clouds away. It warmed her and dried her wet skirt slowly. She felt grubby and toyed with the idea of taking a swim when they watered the horses. But when the river came in sight again, she gave up that notion in a hurry. The water swirled deep and wide, brown with churning mud.

"The water's so high," she gasped, turning in her saddle to speak to Tom.

"Lotta rain last night."

She trotted Kip onward, not daring to canter on the wet strip between the ruts. As the sun rose higher, she felt the promise of another blistering day. How could it have been so cold last night? Sweat beads formed along the inside of her hatband and trickled down her face.

They rode for nearly an hour before coming to another ford. She looked along the riverbank but could see no ferry or raft.

"Wasn't there a ferry or raft here?" she asked Tom as they dismounted.

"It's probably on the other side. Might have been washed away last night."

The horses snorted and tossed their heads at the muddy water.

"What if they won't drink?" Amy asked.

"We'll find a clearer stream sooner or later."

He didn't seem worried, so she decided she wouldn't worry, either, but she took only a swallow from her half-empty canteen in case it had to last her all day.

"Are we going to cross?" She eyed the swirling water doubtfully.

"We'd have to swim the horses."

"The current looks pretty strong." She was afraid, but if he insisted, she would try it.

"We can stay on this side with horses," Tom said. "It's rougher. We'll have to climb those bluffs and go along the top of them. With wagons, it's a lot easier to cross the river again, but I think we'll be all right."

She nodded, grateful to be spared the plunge into the brown torrent.

"All right, let's go," he said. "We'll get up high where we can see and let the horses graze."

They moved back up the muddy trail from the ford, and Amy realized their tracks would be easy to follow now that the rain had stopped.

They climbed steadily up a grassy slope. At the crest she could look back down at the ford and beyond, down the trail a mile or two.

"You stay with them, and I'll stand watch," Tom said, dismounting. He pulled his rifle from the scabbard and dropped Buck's reins. "We won't unsaddle. If you see anything, yell. I'll watch the back trail and the ford."

She sat down on the grass and adjusted her felt hat to shade her face as much as possible. The horses began eating immediately. When Kip had worked his way several yards from Buck, she got up and brought him closer.

After a while, she lay back on the grass and closed her eyes. *I love him*, she thought, then felt guilty and confused. Guilty, because she ought to be thinking about how they could best survive and get help for her father and the garrison at Fort Bridger. Confused, because she still wasn't sure, but it was a captivating thought.

She sent a quick prayer up for her father and his men, then allowed the more pleasant thoughts to take over.

Tom seemed to care about her now and with more than just the care that was his duty, the drive to keep her safe, to honor his promise to her father. She tried to analyze the few times he had touched her. He had thrown her into the saddle twice. That didn't count, she decided. But he had held her hand by the river last night, and in the cabin he had sat beside her, their arms touching, and slept that way all night long. At least she thought he had. When she had awakened, it seemed he was trying to get up without disturbing her. But any two people who were in danger of freezing would probably set convention aside and resort to body heat to keep them alive.

If you're honest, you'll admit you weren't at death's door, her heart argued. *You wouldn't have frozen if he'd curled up on the floor with his own wet blanket.*

He had wanted to be close to her. Hadn't he? Or had she pushed him into it?

She squirmed a little, remembering how she had offered him half the soggy blanket. Had she overstepped the bounds of propriety? Was she leading a man on?

The thought shocked and repelled her. She had always been taught to be modest and discreet. Still, the feelings Tom kindled in her were stronger than anything she had ever felt before. She knew love was more than a feeling, yet she was ready to commit herself to him for the rest of her life. But how did he feel? He would do anything, anything at all, to keep her safe—even die for her. But that was his duty. It didn't mean he loved her.

If he wasn't called upon to die for her in the next twenty-four hours, would he want to go on being with her? Would he *live* for her?

She wasn't at all sure. Thoughts like that had probably never entered his head. He was determined to hand her over to this Colonel Munroe like a packet of dispatches, then ride back to the west, back to his isolation on the Black Fork.

The more she thought about it, the more she was certain that if he knew she was up here on the bluff daydreaming about marrying him, Tom Barkley would probably make that westward journey as soon as possible and laugh at his escape. Scouts were not family men. They thrived on a solitary life in the wilderness.

Still, Tom wasn't the typical scout. He didn't spit tobacco juice or wear mangy buckskins. He didn't let his hair grow down to his shoulders or hang around with the men who drank and gambled when he visited the fort.

"Amy!"

She sat up quickly, pushing her hat back. Tom was running toward her, over the crest of the hill.

"They're heading for the ford. Come on!"

She jumped up and walked quickly toward Kip. She had almost believed the outlaws had given up, that the remainder of their ride would be peaceful.

"Up you go." Once more he lifted her into the saddle and handed her the reins. He was on Buck and had sheathed the rifle in an instant.

"They'll see our trail," she said.

"Yes, but our horses are fresh now. You go first! If you can't follow the trail, just keep the river in sight. Go as fast as you can."

She wheeled Kip eastward and dug her heels into his sides. He didn't need more encouragement but leaped into a run along the top of the bluff, high above the swollen river. She looked back over her shoulder, wishing they had had a quiet moment together. Wishing she had told Tom she loved him, even if he laughed and told her she was a silly girl. Even if he told her he loved someone else, or that she was not attractive to him, or that she was plumb crazy. She wanted him to know. If she was going to die, she wanted to know she had told him.

Tom was riding hard behind her. There was no sign of the three outlaws yet. Kip and Buck would go fast and might outrun their pursuers. Surely Kip could outrun any other horse. Riding him was sheer pleasure, but that pleasure was displaced now by the fear that gripped her.

She rode on, periodically looking back for Buck. When she couldn't see him, she slowed Kip to a trot until the steady buckskin came into view. After a while, she no longer could discern the track. She wasn't sure if she had lost it from not paying attention or if it had just petered out in the scanty clumps of buffalo grass.

She came to a clear creek that cut between six-foot banks, burbling toward the Platte. Kip high-stepped nervously as she walked him along the edge, looking for a place to cross. Finally she found a spot where the bank was less steep, and she thought that if she rode Kip upstream a few yards, he could climb the opposite side.

He plummeted over the edge, and she nearly lost her balance. When he reached the water, he stopped abruptly, stretching his head down for a drink. Amy was flung forward, almost flying over his neck. Her hands shook as she pulled herself upright in the saddle. She let him drink his fill, but Buck was still not in sight when Kip raised his head.

The streambed was rocky, and she let Kip walk slowly, feeling his way. Her eyes scanned the east bank for the best spot to leave the creek.

Where was Tom?

She was frightened. He ought to have reached the creek by now. She urged Kip forward, then forced him toward the bank.

He lunged up and over the top, and she wondered if Buck would be able to do it. She looked back across the stream, and far back she could see the buckskin coming at a dead gallop.

A sudden vision of Buck running unheeding over the creek bank and crashing to the rocky streambed below terrified her, but as the gelding drew closer, he snorted and threw his head.

"Tom! Be careful!" She wasn't sure her voice carried across the gulf between them. The ceaseless prairie wind blew the words back in her face.

"I see it!" His words came faint but distinct as he reined Buck in.

"Follow my trail!"

Buck swerved to the right along the bank toward the place where Kip had leaped down to the water.

Amy caught her breath as Buck scrambled down. He was safe. He stuck his nose down into the stream, but Tom pulled his head up and forced him to trot against the current toward her.

She looked over the creek bed again and saw the reason for his urgency. The three riders were in sight, half a mile back from the creek. Their horses were galloping toward her, and she knew they could see her.

"Tom! Down here!"

Kip pranced along the edge of the embankment. She looked upstream, frantic to find an easier spot for Buck to navigate the bank.

"Ride, Amy!" Tom shouted.

She couldn't make Kip turn and resume his flight until she knew Tom was out of the ravine.

"Don't wait! Ride!" He sounded desperate.

She looked again toward the riders. They were much closer.

Buck lunged at the bank, scrabbling for his footing, and hung momentarily on the edge, fighting for balance. Then he was up and running, past Kip.

Amy turned the gray on his hindquarters and let his reins

out. He needed no command but flew into the gallop that made Amy feel she was flying five feet above the earth.

As he surged past Buck, she cried to Tom, "I lost the trail!"

"Doesn't matter! Keep going!"

❧

Kip was soon leading by several lengths, and Tom saw Amy looking over her shoulder again for Buck. The stalwart buckskin went on, and Tom wondered if his horse would run and run until his heart burst.

Tom didn't need to urge Buck to run. The faithful horse would follow Kip anywhere now. And he would follow Amy. He and Buck were her first and last line of defense. He glanced toward the river. He usually took this stretch on the other side, but he judged they still had eighty miles to go, maybe eighty-five. The terrain was hilly, and he knew more streams would cut through it ahead. Kip was so long-legged, he could probably jump right over the smaller ones. Others, like the one they had just forded, were too wide and cut deep channels that were difficult to cross. Buck would lose ground on those.

He looked behind. The riders had gained a little, and he dug his heels into Buck's ribs, hating to ask more of him when he sensed the horse was already giving his best. He'd trained Buck from the time he was a green colt. They'd been inseparable for four years, and now they were having the ride of their lives.

"Just get through today with me, boy, and I promise you'll live high after this." He slapped Buck's withers, and the gelding snorted and dashed on, chasing Kip. The gray was far ahead now, but Tom knew Amy would pull him in if she got too far out in front. She'd been doing that all morning despite his instructions.

He could understand her fear of going on alone, but she would be safer if she would just forget about him and tear for the fort. It would be easier for him to make a stand when the time came if he knew she would go on without stopping.

But he couldn't be sure she would do that. Somehow, she'd gotten her loyalties and her feelings all mixed up. She was forgetting her father's need and the despair that would come over him if his daughter died on the prairie. She was thinking of T. R. Barkley instead, and that wasn't right. He shouldn't have opened up to her so much, let her see inside him. He ought to be expendable in her view, a means to an end. But she wasn't looking at it that way.

She wouldn't have let Brown go if she'd known the plan. When it came down to it, that had been extremely hard for him, too. But he was in charge, and the hard decisions were up to him. His uncertainty of the night before had vanished. It was clear now what he had to do.

He was ready to do it. For honor's sake, for Major Travis, and mostly for Amy. If God gave him the power, he would save her. If the riders came too close, he would stop and steady himself and prepare to take a bullet. But that Frenchman was going down first.

Ahead he saw Kip leap high. There must be a brook there. Buck charged toward it, and Tom concentrated on the terrain.

That girl! She'd stopped again and was looking back at him, making sure he and Buck made it over.

"Go!" he yelled.

She turned the big gray and started off, staring back at him.

The stream was only six feet wide, the banks a couple of feet deep. Buck could have jumped it if he weren't tired, but Tom didn't take the chance. The horse leaped down into the streambed and stumbled, splashing cold water up Tom's pant legs and over the tops of his boots.

"No drinks now, fella." Up the other bank Buck charged. As they burst up onto the grass above, a rifle shot rang out behind him.

"Go!" Tom breathed.

Amy was looking back, but Kip was running.

✿

A rifle cracked behind her, and Amy flung another glance over her shoulder. Buck was racing toward her, and Tom was still in the saddle, bent low over the pommel.

The three outlaws reached the bank of the brook. They had never been so close, and she could see their beards and the guns they carried pointed forward. Two of them flew over the brook, the man in the red shirt and the big man on the spotted horse. The other horse reared at the bank, then plunged into the water.

Amy turned forward and lay low on Kip's neck. A prayer without words left her heart.

Another shot rang out, and she looked back once more, just in time to see Buck stumble and do a complete somersault, his legs flailing in the air. Tom flew forward and to one side, and she screamed.

ten

Kip quivered, his ears switching back and forth as Amy pulled hard on the reins and circled him at a canter.

"Tom!" she screamed.

Unbelievably, he was on his feet. She saw him run, stooping for his musket, then head toward Buck.

The horse was struggling to rise, but one hind leg wouldn't hold him.

The three riders were close, the paint horse out in front by several yards, but she was closer. She pushed Kip toward Tom.

Tom stood, his feet apart, using Buck as a shield. She saw the smoke from his rifle before she heard the report, and the big man on the paint jerked and tumbled from his saddle. Tom threw his musket down as she reached him and drew his revolver.

Kip stopped so fast he nearly went over backward. The two remaining riders checked momentarily, just out of pistol range.

Tom turned toward her. "You crazy woman! I told you to go!"

She kicked her foot out of the left stirrup, and he jumped up behind her.

"Go!" he yelled in her ear before he was settled.

Kip bounded away. Amy tried to look back, but all she could see was Tom's shoulder and his grim face.

"Are they coming?" she shouted.

"Not yet."

His left arm encircled her waist, and he held her firmly. She pushed Kip on.

"We need to rest," she said after several miles, turning so he could hear her.

She felt him turn in the saddle.

"Find some cover."

They were coming into an area of rock formations. Amy guided Kip between two tall columns and eased him down to a walk.

"Whoa, Kip."

Tom slid down and reached up to catch her as she jumped from the saddle. "Let him breathe."

"He needs water."

"I know. We'll come back to the river after a while. He'll have to wait until then." He detached the canteen from the saddle and handed it to her.

"I'm sorry about Buck."

Tom shrugged, but she knew he felt the loss deeply. She took a small sip of water and offered him the canteen. He took it and put the stopper in without drinking.

"Too bad I couldn't get that other horse."

"Did they stop chasing us?" she asked.

"No. I think they stopped long enough to reload and see if their friend was dead is all."

"Is he?"

"I hit him point blank."

"So what now?"

"Now I get up on that rock over there and watch behind us while you hang on to Kip. If we lose him, we've had it."

She nodded soberly.

His face was like granite as he stood on the boulder, facing west. He'd lost his hat when Buck fell, so he shaded his eyes with one hand. She held Kip's reins, and the horse stood breathing deeply, not seeming to care about the parched grass anymore.

She wanted to ask Tom what they would do if Kip fell, but she didn't want to think about that.

❧

Tom stood immobile, watching, trying not to let his thoughts stray to Buck. Amy led Kip over to the base of the rock. She started to lean against it but jumped away quickly from its fiery hot surface.

"Maybe Buck's leg will heal, and he'll be all right," she ventured.

Tom said nothing. He knew that if the riders hadn't already shot Buck, the wolves would pull him down that night. He should have put a bullet in the horse's head himself, but the thought that he might lose the battle for Amy for the lack of one bullet had held him back.

His left hip and elbow were throbbing from when he'd hit the ground, but he ignored the pain. He needed to prepare Amy to defend herself and find her way to Fort Laramie alone.

"Get that other gun out," he said.

Amy fumbled with the buckle of the saddlebag and produced Layton's gun belt. She held it up to him, stretching and standing on tiptoe.

He glanced down at her, then returned to watching the trail.

"Put it on," he said. "If we're afoot all of a sudden, I don't want to have to stop for it."

She hesitated, then wrapped the belt around her waist. Although Layton had been a thin man, it was far too large. She took it off and tried slinging it over her shoulder, but it slipped awkwardly down her arm. When they were riding, it would be worse, Tom knew.

"Give it here." He took out his hunting knife and cut six inches from the leather strap, then bored a new hole in the belt.

"Try that." He put the belt and holster in her hand, then stood up again to watch the trail while she put it on.

"That's better."

"All right. How's Kip doing?"

"He's got his wind back, I think."

Tom hopped down from the rock and prepared to boost her into the saddle again.

"Wait," she said, putting one hand out against his chest. "You take the saddle. I'll ride behind you."

"No."

"Why not?"

He looked down into her vivid blue eyes, wanting to shield her from the stark truth. But she had to know what they were up against. "That saddle was made for you. It won't fit me. Besides, the enemy is behind us, and I'm not going to expose your back as a target."

She swallowed hard, and he thought she would argue. He'd seen that stubborn glint in the major's eyes.

Tom was trying to hold his wits together. The danger to him and Amy had carried him through the fall and the hasty parting with Buck, but that rush of energy had dissipated, and fear was closing in. He had thrown the musket down after he'd fired it, knowing he didn't have time to salvage the lead for it from Buck's saddlebags. Now he couldn't shoot back unless their enemies came close. At least they had Layton's extra powder and ammunition for the revolvers in Kip's saddlebags.

Seconds counted, and he couldn't let his feelings for Amy slow him down. He tried to glare down at her, to stop her from protesting further, but he couldn't.

"We're wasting time, Amy," he said softly.

She was still looking up at him, but she wasn't angry.

"All right." She put her hand up for an instant to his jaw.

He was tempted to scoop her into his arms, but that wouldn't keep them alive. She turned away almost immediately, reaching for the stirrup. Again he picked her up and settled her gently on Kip's back. She pushed her legs forward of the leathers, and he got his left foot in the stirrup and swung up behind her.

He looked off to the west. Was that a puff of alkali dust on the trail? He couldn't be sure. Mirages were common in this territory. The rainwater had kept the dust down all morning, but it had soaked into the ground, and the sun had done its work. If it was their pursuers, he judged them to be a mile away.

He put his arms around Amy's waist, holding her with his left hand and grasping the saddle horn with his right. Amy squeezed Kip, and the horse took off again at a canter.

❧

Half an hour later, they came to another clear stream, and Tom made Amy stop Kip with the horse's forefeet in the water.

"You stay up there, but let him drink," Tom said, sliding down to give Kip a respite from his weight. "If I tell you to go and I'm still on the ground, you go, you hear me?"

He scowled into her eyes, and her lower lip trembled.

"I hear you," she whispered.

He nodded and went around to the off side and unbuckled the saddlebag.

"Here." He thrust a piece of dried beef into her hand. "Eat."

While she chewed, he took out the bag of lead balls and put half a dozen in the pocket of his trousers, then stuffed as many powder cartridges and caps in his shirt pocket as would fit. He closed the saddlebag and took the canteen, stooping to fill it.

Kip's throat made gulping sounds as he swallowed.

Tom looked up at Amy. She turned away quickly, but he saw tears in her eyes. He handed her the canteen, and she tipped it up for a drink then handed it back.

"Drink more," he commanded.

She did. He took it and filled it, then stoppered it and secured it on the back of the saddle.

"Should we drop the blanket and saddlebags?" There was a tremor in her voice.

Tom hesitated. Ounces as well as seconds counted.

"We need the lead and powder. If you want to drop the blanket and your personal things, do it now. I'll take a look behind us."

He scrambled back up the western bank of the rivulet. No riders and no dust clouds were within sight, but because of the undulating prairie, he couldn't be sure they weren't close.

"Take Kip up the far bank and wait for me," he called.

She obeyed, and Tom descended to the stream again, crossing over on foot, hopping from rock to rock, then scrambled up the low bank on the east side to where she waited.

She took her foot from the stirrup, and he swung up into his former position behind her on Kip's back, one arm tight around her waist.

"Let's go," he said quietly in her ear.

It was too hot to be so close to another person, but he didn't care. Little droplets of sweat clung to the back of her neck below the hat brim, where her hair was tied. He hoped he would live to be this close to her again, when he didn't have to think about keeping her alive. Whether he died today or fifty years from now, he would always remember how small her waist was and how incongruous the thick leather gun belt felt just below the waistband of her dusty split skirt.

&

They rode on. Kip seemed to have found new energy and maintained the rocking-chair canter for some time. When he slowed of his own accord, they continued at a trot.

Amy drooped beneath the searing sun. They ought to stop in the shade somewhere. She jerked awake. Tom's arm tightened just a little around her middle.

"It's all right," he whispered, his breath tickling her ear, and she realized she'd nodded off and was leaning back against his chest.

She ought to be embarrassed, but she wasn't. Even though she was in mortal danger, she felt safe. She put her right hand over Tom's on the saddle horn, and he gripped her fingers.

"You ought to have left me back there," he murmured.

"Never." She turned her head against his chest, and her hat shifted. "Take my hat," she said.

"It won't fit me."

She was wide awake now. "Are you all right?"

"Yes. A little stiff. How about you?"

"I'm tired."

"I could tell," he chuckled.

"Do you think they're still after us?"

"Yes. We have to keep moving until we meet someone or reach the fort."

She hadn't thought of meeting a detachment or an emigrant train. They hadn't met anyone going west since the troopers' camp. But it was late in the season, as Tom had pointed out.

"How far now?" she asked.

"I don't know. Sixty or seventy miles, maybe. I don't think they'll chase us right up to the fort. If this horse can keep going, we may outrun them yet."

"I knew he was special," she said dreamily.

"He's incredible," Tom said.

She laid her head back against him, the hat brim coming far down, almost to her eyes. She wished she could stay in his arms always, sweaty and tired as he was. She herself had never felt so filthy. If they made it to Fort Laramie, the second thing she would do was take a bath. The first would be to tell Tom Barkley she loved him.

That would be the appropriate time, she decided, unless it looked like they were going to die short of the fort.

For the moment, she had hope. Kip was still moving, and Tom was holding her in his arms. Not by his own choice, it was true, but she thought his touch was more tender than was absolutely necessary. And he still held her fingers. He didn't have to.

When this was over and they didn't have to keep close company, she would see if he still wanted to be near her. Maybe he was just trying to keep her from giving up. She hoped it was more than that.

eleven

Another ford. They had worked their way down from the high prairie to the level of the river, and now the wagon road would be on the south bank again.

"I want to swim!" she cried.

Tom laughed, hopping down from Kip's back.

"In that filthy river? It's just thin mud."

"I'm so hot!"

He guessed he was partly to blame for that. He hadn't needed to hold her so tightly, could have let some air get between them.

"Can I at least get down?" she asked.

"All right, but keep your boots on." He lifted her down. Kip was settling for the muddy water this time. When the horse lifted his head, Tom led him away from the river to get a view down the trail.

Amy followed them. She was still beautiful, though her skirt was spattered and stained and the back and sides of her blouse were soaked with perspiration. Her face was streaked with dirt. She took her hat off and mopped her forehead with her sleeve as she walked toward him. He smiled.

"What's funny?" she asked when she was close. "Am I so filthy my own father wouldn't recognize me?"

"Just about," he laughed. The skin of his bottom lip split, and he sucked it. "Can't wait 'til we get some of that lard."

She laughed, too. "We're two of the dirtiest people in the territory, I'm sure. I don't know as they'll let us in the gate at Fort Laramie."

"Up you go." He reached to lift her. He stopped with his hands on her waist. He usually waited until she turned toward the horse to get the stirrup, but this time he'd reached for her while she still faced him.

You're crazy! he told himself. *You can't kiss a woman when the people who want to kill you could pop up any second.* But he wanted to very much.

"Tom."

He swallowed. He really ought to speak to the major before he made advances to his daughter. Besides, his lip was bleeding, and hers were in rough shape, too. Would a kiss like that be pleasant? He'd never kissed a woman, and he didn't want it to be torture when he did.

"We'd better move."

She nodded, still looking up at him, and he wondered what she had been about to say. In her eyes there seemed to be something that answered the deep longing in his heart. Her breath came out in a little puff, and she turned toward Kip. Tom lifted her carefully, then climbed up behind her and slid his arms around her. He turned Kip so he could look down the trail, then headed east again.

❧

They kept moving for two hours. Tom wouldn't let the hope rise in him that their pursuers had given up. Kip was jogging slowly, his head drooping a little. *As long as he keeps moving,* Tom thought. *Just keep moving.*

The wagon trail was dry, and he doubted the rain had touched this section. Occasional puffs of breeze swirled their own dust around them, making Amy cough and choke. Tom's eyes smarted, and every muscle in his body ached, but he held on to her, and he thought she actually slept for a few minutes, slumped against him, limp and soft.

They came to the bank of a wide stream that had cut a deep gash in the prairie, and he stopped Kip on the edge, looking back for a minute before they descended the slope to the water.

Amy leaned back against him to help the horse balance as he

went down the incline. The water was up to Kip's knees, and he stood in it, drinking as though he would empty the stream.

"He's so tired," Amy moaned.

"I know. He's done more than I ever expected he could."

"Should we stop for a while?"

"We should, but. . ." He glanced uneasily over his shoulder. He couldn't see beyond the bank where the wagon road rose several feet.

"How far?" she asked in a small voice.

"Fifty miles. They say this stream is fifty miles out from the fort. I think it's a little less, actually."

"That's good. We're really going to make it, Tom."

"Well. . ." He was noncommittal. Between them and Fort Laramie was a rugged range of stony hills supporting scrub pines and juniper. He knew the rocky country would be hard on a horse already pressed to the limits of endurance.

"What?" Amy asked. "You said they won't chase us right up to the fort."

"Right, so. . ."

"What aren't you telling me?" She swiveled around and stared at him searchingly.

"So they'll want to make their move soon, before we get too close to Fort Laramie."

Her eyes grew large, and he hated frightening her.

"If Kip could rest for an hour or two, he could carry us all that way," she said.

"Maybe. But. . . " He looked west again, and it bothered him that he couldn't see out of the streambed. He ought to have waited up above while she watered the horse. "Let's get up out of here, and I'll walk for a while and give Kip a break."

"I'll walk, too," she said immediately.

"No."

"Why not?"

"You don't weigh much."

"But he needs the rest."

Tom grimaced and took the reins, pulling Kip's head up. "You've got to stay on him," he said as the gray waded across the water. It came up to the stirrups. Amy lifted her feet up along the horse's neck.

Kip heaved up the far bank, and Tom pulled on the reins and jumped down, staggering as he landed. Walking would do his stiff muscles good.

"I want to walk, too," Amy insisted.

"No."

"Why?"

"You know why." He walked alongside the horse. She said nothing, but after a few minutes, he began to worry. She was so headstrong, and she had come charging back for him when Buck fell.

"You listen to me," he said sternly. "If I tell you to go, you go."

"You've said that before."

"And you didn't always do it."

"Tom. . ." She sounded helpless and hurt.

"I'm serious. Kip needs to rest now, and this is the best plan I can think of. If they don't show up, I'll keep walking. If they do, I'll jump on again. But if there's no time and I tell you, girl, you get out of here. You hear me? Ride straight to the fort. Don't stop for anything. Not anything."

She set her chin stubbornly and refused to look at him.

"Promise," he said threateningly.

He thought she sniffed. How could she have enough moisture in her body to cry?

"Amy," he warned.

"I promise," she said bitterly.

"All right." He was not completely mollified. "We've evened the odds somewhat. If they still think they need to do this, I'll do everything I can to make sure they don't get past me. But it's God you should count on, Amy. Not me."

They trudged along in silence for half an hour. Slightly past its apex, the sun beat down cruelly. Every time they topped a rise, Tom turned and looked back, shielding his eyes and squinting. Nothing. He turned and walked on beside the tall gray horse.

If the outlaws never came again, so be it. They would go on slowly. If he walked the last fifty miles, that was all right, too, so long as Amy got there alive. But he really thought they would meet someone soon, now that they were on the last stretch of the wagon trail. The Indians in these parts were generally friendly. They would certainly help them get to the fort. Or a detachment of troopers might be out patrolling. A trader might still be heading for Fort Hall or Fort Bridger with supplies for the winter.

They saw no one, unless three pronghorns and a small colony of prairie dogs counted.

Tom realized he'd been plodding along in the wagon rut for some time without checking behind. They were climbing a long, gradual slope. He glanced uneasily over his left shoulder.

Was it dust, or was it a trick of the sun? Maybe a breeze had stirred and raised a puff of alkali. He stopped, and after a few steps, Kip stopped, too.

"Tom?" Amy called, her voice rising.

He walked slowly to the horse, looking back as he went.

"Do you see dust?" He felt stupid and sluggish.

She looked hard to the west, craning her neck.

"I see it."

"Come on." He started walking again.

"Tom!" She was shouting at him urgently. "Get on the horse, Tom!"

She sidled Kip up next to him, and her leg and the stirrup brushed against his shoulder.

"Get up!" she cried.

That jolted him, and he was able to act. He seized Kip's bridle and jumped up behind Amy. As soon as he landed, she kicked Kip into a trot, and the horse labored to the top of the long hill.

"Turn around," Tom said.

She turned the horse, and they sat staring down the trail.

The dust cloud was nearer, and he thought he could make out a horse.

"It might not be them." There was no hope in her voice.

Tom reached the left rein and pulled Kip's head around. He squeezed him hard, and the gray began to trot.

❧

Amy's mind was whirling. She had let herself believe they were done with it in spite of Tom's dire predictions.

"Maybe we could hide somewhere until they get close and see if it's really them," she said, turning to speak close to his ear.

"No. I don't have a rifle. The only way I'll do that is if you'll keep going without me."

"No," she said flatly. He was right. The best plan, the only reasonable plan, was to keep going.

They were over the crest of the hill, and Tom was constantly twisting to look back.

"What are you thinking?" she yelled.

"Nothing that would work."

Kip cantered on across the prairie. Tom sat still behind Amy, keeping his weight centered as much as possible, and let her guide the horse. As they climbed another long hill, Kip slowed to a jog. Tom looked back and caught his breath.

"What is it?" Amy asked.

"The paint horse. I shot his rider, but they're bringing the extra horse along."

She put her hand over his where he clutched her waist, and she felt his grip tighten for an instant. She didn't say anything, but she grasped the implication. The riders were close enough that Tom could make out two horsemen and a horse with an empty saddle. They had a remount and could alternate the horses. She and Tom, meanwhile, had one horse to carry them both.

She squeezed Kip a little more, and he halfheartedly broke into a canter again.

"I'm sorry, Kip," she whispered.

"You say something?" Tom's voice was loud in her ear.

She shook her head and blinked at the tears that kept coming. She needed to be able to see. *I'm sorry, Daddy*, she cried inwardly. *Tom's done his best. He really has.*

She knew she was crying out to the wrong person. Her breath was coming in gasps, and she tried to steady it. This was not the time to lose control. She was able at last to form a prayer.

Dear Lord, please help us. I know You're the only One who can. And whatever happens, don't let Father blame Tom. She gulped and fought the urge to turn around again. *Let us live, dear God. But if that's not what You want, let me be strong to the end.*

Tom drew his Colt revolver. "Amy, remember, God is with you." His lips touched her right ear.

She nodded.

"You keep going, no matter what." His arms tightened around her.

Now is the time, she thought. *It's not the appropriate time, but it's the only time.*

She leaned back hard against his chest and turned her face toward his neck. "Tom, I love you."

"Amy!" It was little more than a sob.

A rifle cracked behind them, and Kip leaped forward, faster.

❧

Tom's adrenaline surged. They still had a chance. Their pursuers couldn't reload while riding.

"Keep going," he said relentlessly. "That's one musket discharged. If they keep missing, we'll be down to handguns, and we'll be even again."

Of course, they had three rifles, maybe four if they'd picked up his. More if they'd gotten Layton's and Brown's.

He wouldn't think about that.

She loved him. She had dared to say that. Maybe it was just some misplaced surge of emotion for her protector, a panicky declaration she would regret later. He wished there was time to think about it, to savor it, but there was none. He knew vaguely that it was something he couldn't hold her to later, even though his own heart told him he loved her, too.

His legs were very tired from clinging to the horse without stirrups, and he could only hold on with one hand now, since he'd drawn the pistol. It took all his concentration to stay on Kip's back.

He looked back and saw the red-shirted Frenchman dropping back and swinging his leg over the paint horse's saddle without stopping. Meanwhile, the man in buckskins edged forward on a long-legged bay.

Tom felt a wave of despair. They were close, too close. He tried to level the pistol at them, but it would be hopeless to shoot turning backward while Kip was galloping and the targets were moving, too.

"You'll have a better chance without me." He'd been thinking it for some time now, but he'd known she wouldn't like it.

"No, Tom! Don't leave me!"

Her cry was so piteous, it wrenched his heart.

"I can jump and make a stand. You keep going."

"No!"

"We knew it might come to this," he said in her ear.

"No!" she shouted again. "Don't do it!"

Another shot split the air, and even as Amy heard it, she felt Tom's hold loosen. He slipped back over Kip's hindquarters, sliding down the left side.

"Tom!" she screamed. She looked back and was terrified to see him lying on the trail behind her. He didn't jump up and run as he had when Buck went down.

Instead of hesitating, Kip leaped forward with the lessening of weight on his back and charged on up the hillside.

twelve

Tom hit the ground hard and lay staring up at blue sky. The sound of Kip's hoofbeats receded. He had planned to jump off but not quite that soon. Had he lost his balance? He was winded, stunned by the fall. He struggled to breathe deeply. It hurt. When he tried to sit up, fierce pain stabbed through his left shoulder. He knew he was hit and hoped the bullet was high enough to have missed the lung.

With a shock, he realized the two riders were almost on top of him, and he looked around frantically for his pistol. The bay horse charged toward him, and he thought he would be run over, but the man in buckskins pulled the horse up sharply, and the bay stopped, his front hooves landing within inches of Tom's head.

Tom forced himself to a sitting position, but the trapper leaned over from the saddle, pointing his musket at Tom.

"Well, Barkley. Here we are at last."

The Frenchman flew past on the pinto, dropping the reins of the third mount, a brown with white stockings, and Tom looked quickly after him. The pinto was twenty yards behind Kip. Amy must have hesitated again.

God, give her wings.

He knew his prayer was futile.

The trapper leaped down from the bay horse and stood over him, his gun barrel almost touching Tom's chest. His dirty blond hair hung in clumps beneath a battered hat.

"I don't know why you're still alive." The man showed his teeth in a grudging smile. "Say, maybe we'd better fix that."

Tom tried to sit still, staring up at him, not twitching a muscle. His mind was racing. They had fired two muskets.

He couldn't see another on the bay's saddle. Surely the outlaw wouldn't hold an empty gun on him? Or would he?

The man's hand moved slightly toward the trigger, just as a scream rent the air from above them on the hillside.

It was enough of a distraction for the man with the rifle. His glance flickered toward the hilltop, and Tom seized the end of the barrel, yanking it hard to one side and forward.

The explosion was deafening next to his ear, and the trapper's eyes were wide with surprise as he tried to maintain his grip on the musket.

Tom pulled and twisted with an effort that wrenched his shoulder violently, but with Amy's life at stake, he ignored the pain. He had the gun now. It was empty, but he swung it by the barrel, aiming for the man's knees.

The trapper hopped back, taking the blow on the shin. He swore and stood sizing Tom up, his eyes glittering.

"Well, now," he said evenly. Slowly he reached for his belt.

I'm dead, Tom thought. *He's got a pistol, and I'm dead. God, help Amy. Don't leave her unprotected.*

Even as his prayer went up, Tom rose carefully to his feet. He dropped the musket and reached for his hunting knife.

He almost laughed when his adversary pulled out his own blade. They were even now, except for Tom's wound and Amy's heart-wrenching screams that made his heart race.

He wanted so badly to look toward her but didn't dare take his gaze off the man whose wolfish eyes glinted at him.

Tom circled slowly until he was facing the hillside. Way at the top, he saw in one quick glance that Kip was riderless, skittering nervously sideways, his reins dangling. The brown horse was cropping grass halfway up the hillside, and the pinto was at the top near Kip. Tom glimpsed the red-shirted man, still in the saddle, against the dark background of the pines, holding Amy half on and half off the horse. He had an impression of flailing limbs and a gleam of light off Amy's golden hair, streaming loose.

He riveted his eyes on his immediate adversary. Amy was putting up a fight. It wasn't over yet. He had a score to settle here before he could finish matters.

"I almost called it quits after you shot Ollie," the man said, his smile a snarl. "That made LeBeau really mad, though. He and Ollie were great pals."

Tom's mind tried to process everything, the man's position, his movements, his words. He said nothing, saving his breath and concentrating, thinking how he could speed things up and come out the victor.

The trapper leaped at him suddenly, and Tom deflected the thrust of the knife with his left arm, tripping the man up and crashing to the ground with him. A jolt of pain ran through his injured shoulder. Somehow they landed beneath the bay horse, and the gelding sidestepped gingerly, whinnying in protest. Tom rolled away, and the other man ducked away from the horse, then groped about on the ground. Tom realized he was searching for his knife.

It was the opening Tom needed. He lunged, slicing hard as he brought the man to the ground again. The tough buckskin slowed the blade, and Tom didn't think he'd hurt him much. They struggled, face-to-face on the ground, both determined to control Tom's knife.

Tom's weakened left arm was giving way. The trapper kneed him in the stomach, then rolled away with the knife in his hand.

Tom rose to his knees, fighting nausea. He was in so much pain, he didn't know if he could stand up again. As he tried, he focused, slowly, agonizingly, on a metallic object just inches from his left hand—the pistol he had dropped when he fell from the horse.

He looked away from it quickly. If the other man noticed, Tom would have less of a chance.

The trapper was crouching, weaving slightly, looking for an opening. He was just about to leap when Tom grabbed the revolver and whipped it up, squeezing the trigger.

Click.

The man's eyes widened in surprise, then he smiled.

"Forget to reload, sonny?"

Tom's heart sank. *God, I tried so hard to keep the pistols dry.* In that instant, he knew he must cock the pistol and squeeze the trigger five more times. All six chambers couldn't misfire.

As the man came toward him, Tom aimed at his face, but before he could pull the hammer back again, the hang fire caught, and the powder exploded in the chamber with a roar. The man flew backward, and Tom stood staring, feeling sick.

❧

Amy screamed when the man in the red shirt galloped up beside her and tried to pull her from the saddle. She dug into Kip's sides, and he leaped with a squeal, but the man's grip was like iron. She kicked free of the stirrups and tried to leap off the far side, but the man yanked her from Kip's saddle and pulled her to him. Amy shrieked.

She kicked and writhed as he struggled to pull her onto his horse. When he clapped a hand over her mouth, she bit him fiercely.

He swore, and Amy tumbled to the ground. Dazed, she got to her feet and backed away from the pinto, then turned and ran toward the tree line. The spotted horse thundered behind her. Suddenly, the ground dropped away, and she found herself sliding down a steep slope into a cleft between the hills. She grabbed at a small pine branch, and the needles sliced her palms, but she held on and stopped her descent.

Above her, the pinto balked, and she heard the man cursing in French. She eased to her feet and tried to move down the slope without sliding again, but her boots slipped, and she sat down hard. Below her, the slope was near vertical with a drop of five feet over the face of a ledge. She looked to the sides but saw no prospect of better footing.

Branches snapped above her, and she looked up. LeBeau

had left the horse and was following her down cautiously. A huge lump blocked her throat, and she couldn't scream anymore. There seemed to be no escape.

She reached for the pistol she wore at her side and pulled it clumsily from the holster.

"Go away," she tried to shout, but it came out a whisper.

She raised the gun with shaking hands and struggled to pull the hammer back.

The Frenchman was just above her, holding on to a tree root and reaching out, the sleeve of his red shirt stretching toward her.

Amy pulled the trigger and felt herself falling from the rock as the concussion shook the air in the ravine. She dropped the pistol and tried to extend her arms, but the ground rushed up too fast. Her ankles took the first shock of the landing, but she couldn't gain her balance. She stumbled forward, knowing she was going to hit hard, but she couldn't stop.

⬥

Tom realized Amy's screams had stopped, and as the ringing in his ears receded, it was eerily quiet. The brown horse was trotting away to the south, around the side of the hill. He could see Kip and the bay but not the pinto.

He pulled his knife from the trapper's lifeless hand, shoved the revolver in his holster, and ran up the hill. When he came near Kip, he stopped, looking all around and panting. Had they gone over the hill?

A muffled report came from his right, and he ran toward it to where the side of the hill fell away steeply and the trees began. He saw the pinto halfway down the draw, his saddle empty.

"Amy!" he shouted.

There was no answer. He worked his way carefully down the steep hillside, grasping the trunks of the scrub pines to keep from plummeting down the slope. The pain in his shoulder alternately stabbed and ached, and he wondered if he would be able to climb up the hill again. As he came even with the pinto, it eyed him balefully and went on snatching at the meager grass.

"Amy!"

He listened.

A rustling sounded below where the brush was thick. He drew the revolver.

"LeBeau!" he called.

"Halt! Come no closer, Barkley."

Tom stood still, homing in on the voice. "What do you want, LeBeau?"

There was a short laugh. "I have what I want, monsieur, although it has cost me dear."

"Give me the girl. I'll give you whatever you want."

"I do not think that is in your power."

"Do you want money?" Tom asked, taking a cautious step.

"Alas, money will not buy my brother's life."

Tom took another step. "Your brother is the man Major Travis arrested at Fort Bridger."

"Eh, bien. You see my difficulty."

"LeBeau, we can work this out." Tom took two steps. He was on top of a granite ledge, and the voice came from the shadows below.

"I told you, stay away. This young lady will ride with me, and I am sure you want her to be in good health when she goes."

Tom thought he saw a tuft of red in the shade of the thick pines, but the sun was setting, and he couldn't be sure. He crouched behind an outcropping of the ledge.

It struck him suddenly that LeBeau might not even have her. Perhaps she had escaped him after all. "Amy?" he called cautiously.

LeBeau laughed derisively. "The young lady does not wish to speak to gentlemen callers just now."

"Where is she, LeBeau?"

"That I cannot tell you."

Fear coursed through him. He looked toward the pinto, where it grazed on the slope. A rifle stuck up from a scabbard on the saddle.

"Can't or won't?"

"She is. . .with me. But you must go away. Take the big gray horse and ride to the fort if you wish. Get reinforcements and chase me across the territory, the way I chased you. But I will get to Fort Bridger before you do, and I will do my business with the major."

"What business?"

"It is a tiresome thing. I have what the major wants, you see, and he has what I want."

"Your brother."

"Yes. We can make a trade. The major would not take money to release my brother, I am certain. But he will accept the gift of his daughter's life."

"You were on your way to Fort Bridger when we passed the troopers' camp," Tom said, reaching out with his foot and feeling the edge of the rock.

"I was going to plead with the major to release him. But when I learned the perfect persuasion was within reach. . . Monsieur, let us say I did not expect it to take so long to fetch my trade goods."

As he spoke, Tom leaned forward toward the rim of the ledge, judging the distance to the ground below.

"Get back! I insist, monsieur."

Tom sat still. "It seems to me that if you had a gun, you'd have used it by now."

"Oh, you think I have no weapons?" LeBeau laughed. "Are you forgetting the army pistol the young lady so kindly brought me? Here, I will show you."

The report was loud in the canyon, and chips flew up from the rock that was partly shielding Tom. The pinto snorted and jumped several feet up the steep side of the draw. Tom dove low behind the scant cover and called, "All right! You have a gun. Let's talk."

LeBeau laughed again. "I did not think you were a man who liked to talk. You have killed my friend Oliver, and now I assume that you have also killed Martin. Otherwise, you would not be here. No, Barkley, you are a man who acts, not a man who talks. I am telling you now, leave at once, or I will kill you."

"No. I'm sworn to protect Amy Travis. I'm not leaving here without her."

"I will not hurt the young lady. I will merely return her to her father."

"I don't trust you."

"Ah, that is most unfortunate."

"Let's deal," said Tom.

"What could you have that I could possibly want?" asked the mocking voice.

"You've gotten separated from your horses."

"It is true. This little spitfire led me on a chase and tried to blow my brains out, as you say, but I have her now. I do not see that you have the horses."

"I can keep you from getting to them."

"And I can keep you from Miss Travis. So?"

Tom sat still, thinking. "I'll give you any horse you want and whatever food there is."

"How would this help my brother?"

"It wouldn't, but nothing will help your brother now. Either the major's hanged him or he's let him go."

"I think not," said LeBeau.

"You have communication with Fort Bridger?"

"In a sense. I gave the army corporal a sealed letter for the major before I left his camp. I did not divulge my purpose, but I told him to put this letter in Major Travis's hand, no other. In the letter, I told the major that if he wished to see his daughter alive again, he would release Raymond LeBeau."

"He won't do it."

"You don't think he will? Not immediately, perhaps, but neither will he hang him. When I return to Fort Bridger with proof that his daughter is in my custody, he will reconsider."

"What if Major Travis won't bargain with you?"

"Ah, *elle est belle.* I can find another use for her, I think. I shall not lose on this enterprise."

Tom clenched his fingers around the butt of his pistol, trying to control the rage that filled him. "You're going to need more help than your brother does. You've kidnapped a woman and killed a soldier."

LeBeau said nothing, and the silence lengthened.

"LeBeau?" Tom called. There was no answer. He poised again on the edge of the rock and jumped down, then ran to the thicket, pushing through the branches, stumbling over roots.

In the dusk, he saw the Frenchman moving slowly ahead of him, dragging Amy backward by her upper arms.

"Hold it!" Tom aimed his revolver at LeBeau.

LeBeau pulled Amy up and crouched with her in his arms, producing his own pistol.

"I think it is the standoff, monsieur."

Tom ducked back into the brush. He realized he was shaking. Blood was streaming down LeBeau's right cheek, congealing in his beard, and Amy appeared to be unconscious. "You've hurt her."

"No, no, monsieur. She is a wild little thing. She hurt herself—after she tried to kill me."

Tom swallowed, not sure what to believe, but he knew one thing. "I'm not letting you take her."

"Then we have nothing to say." LeBeau raised his pistol and fired. The ball whizzed past Tom's ear. He jumped back into the thicket and stood still, thinking.

He turned and crept up the slope as quietly as he could. Bit by bit, he worked his way up the side of the canyon toward the horse that was now near the top.

The pinto was wary. He'd worked hard all day and wouldn't like the acrid smell of gunpowder that clung to Tom's clothes. When Tom came close, the horse turned his hindquarters toward him and kept eating. Time after time, Tom tried to approach, but the horse was too crafty. At last Tom managed to chase him up the slope and onto the hillside.

Kip was grazing near where Tom had last seen him. Tom whistled, the way he had for Buck so many times, and Kip raised his head and looked at him, then ambled toward him. Tom was so thankful he could have cried.

When the gray reached him, Tom stroked his nose.

"All right, boy, we've got a little more work to do."

He climbed wearily into the saddle, wincing at the pain in his shoulder. He thought he could see the bay gelding far down the hill beyond where he had fought Martin.

The pinto first. He walked Kip slowly toward the animal, one step at a time. The pinto watched distrustfully. Tom edged the gray in, closer and closer, then made a desperate grab for the trailing reins. The pinto wheeled, kicked at Kip, and galloped down the hill.

Tom grimaced. "If that's the way you want it."

He would shoot the pinto before he would leave him for LeBeau. But first he'd go after the bay.

He trotted Kip down the hill, skirting the body of the man in buckskins. The bay let him approach, and Tom soon grasped his reins. He climbed down and took Kip's hobbles from the saddlebag, glad Amy hadn't discarded them with her blanket and dirty clothes. He fitted the straps around the bay's cannons and removed the bridle, then took Amy's decorative saddle off Kip and stood it on its pommel. Throwing the trapper's saddle on Kip, he left the bay grazing contentedly.

The sun had disappeared, and he could not see the brown horse, but he remembered that it had moved away to the south earlier. Time to deal with the pinto.

As Kip jogged toward him, the spotted horse began to trot,

too. As the gray gained ground on him, the pinto broke into a run. Tom clucked, and Kip tore after the smaller horse, flying over the prairie. The pinto dodged away, but Kip stuck to his tail and managed to ease up beside him again.

Patience, Tom told himself. He blocked LeBeau and Amy from his mind and concentrated on the crafty horse, trying to predict which way he would veer next.

At last Kip was running next to the animal, inching up until Tom was even with the pinto's head and could seize one rein. Tom slowed Kip gradually. The pinto pulled at the bit, lunging and squealing.

"Calm down," Tom said quietly. "You're making it hard on yourself. Settle down."

At last the pinto stood quivering, and Tom was able to reach over and claim the other rein. After that, the gelding trotted meekly behind Kip. Tom led him back to where the bay was hobbled. He got down and searched the packs from the trappers' two horses, holding the pinto's reins firmly all the time. Coffee, a frying pan, clothing, and lead. He was rewarded at last with a length of cotton rope and a picket pin.

He improvised a rope halter for the fractious pinto, then took off the saddle and bridle and picketed the animal. If LeBeau made it up out of the steep ravine with Amy while Tom was looking for the brown horse, the Frenchman would find no bridles for the two grazing horses. Tom put them both in Kip's saddlebags.

The darkness deepened as he rode Kip swiftly around the base of the hill to the south, hoping to find the last of the trappers' three mounts.

Kip whinnied and was answered by a shrill neigh from the darkness ahead.

It was so easy, Tom would have laughed if his thoughts hadn't gravitated back to Amy. She'd been unconscious, he was sure. LeBeau must have struck her. Or perhaps she had fallen, as he'd said.

But Tom had all four horses. Maybe LeBeau would bargain now. If not, Tom would shoot two of the animals. He thought he would keep the bay; it seemed the most tractable. One way or another, he and Amy would be riding into Fort Laramie.

As he rode back to the other horses, he planned his next move. He had to get to Amy as quickly as possible, but he couldn't afford to let LeBeau get past him in the darkness and get to the mounts.

Quickly Tom dropped the brown's saddle with the others and tied the three extra horses together. Riding Kip, he led the animals toward the river and down over the bank. While they all drank, he chewed some jerky he'd found in the pinto's saddlebags.

He trotted the horses upstream half a mile. Around a bend, he found a strip of dry grass ten yards wide between the Platte and the high bank. Tom picketed the pinto there and hobbled the bay and LeBeau's brown gelding. It was the best he could do. Unless the Frenchman was already following him, it would take him awhile to locate the mounts, and their saddles were back near where Martin lay.

Tom was bone weary, and he knew Kip was, too, but the big horse obeyed him eagerly when he turned back toward the long hillside and Amy. She was out there somewhere.

Tom didn't let himself speculate about Amy's condition but prayed earnestly that God would protect her and comfort her and give him the wit and strength he would need to win her back from LeBeau.

Grimly, he headed Kip up the hill. He held a loaded musket in his hand, and a second was ready in the saddle scabbard. He had his revolver at his side and his knife in his boot top. Was it enough?

thirteen

Amy awakened in darkness. She hurt. She lay on her side, and as she tried to move, her head throbbed with pain. She couldn't move her hands. It left her feeling very stupid and ill. At last she realized her wrists and ankles were bound, and she trembled with cold and fear. The wind softly stirred the branches above her. Far in the distance, a wolf howled. Closer, she was sure she heard another sound that was not the wind but a regular breathing. When a snore came, she was certain. She began to pray in desperation.

Dear God, let Tom live! No matter what happens to me, let Tom survive!

She had fallen. She had fired the pistol, lost her balance, and tumbled from the ledge. That was all she could remember.

She wiggled her fingers, and the cord that held her hands behind her bit into her wrists. Tears came, unstoppable. She tried to cry silently, but a sob escaped her parched throat.

The Frenchman came and stood over her. She knew it was him. She could smell him, and in a rush she remembered his hands on her, dragging her from Kip's saddle.

"Mademoiselle is awake?"

She said nothing, but he reached down and grabbed her arm, pulling her to a sitting position. There was a bit of moonlight, and she could see a glimmer of lust in his eyes.

"You would be beautiful if you were cleaned up." He reached toward her face.

"Don't touch me," she whispered fiercely.

He laughed. "Still kicking? You must learn to be gentle. Ladies are meant to be amiable."

"Never," she hissed.

He shrugged. "Sometimes it is like the training of a horse, yes?" His hand grazed her cheek, and his fingers settled on her neck.

"You are a filthy murderer. I hate you."

His face darkened. He drew back his hand and struck her.

Amy gasped and cowered, trying not to sob aloud.

LeBeau was breathing heavily. "Sometimes it takes awhile," he said after a moment.

"Tom will kill you."

"Monsieur Barkley? I think not. He is dead, you see."

She felt a deep weight settle on her chest, crushing her.

LeBeau shrugged. "You must not blame me. My friend Martin had to defend himself."

"I don't believe you!"

"As you wish. I will take you at first light to see where he lies." He reached for his belt and began to unbuckle it.

Amy's heart pounded. "My father will hang you." It was a faint whisper.

He laughed. "No, no, he will thank me for bringing him his beautiful daughter. But I must be sure you stay with me until you have learned that I am not so bad. Pardon the indelicacy, but I must ask you to sit over here."

He pulled her to a small pine tree.

"There, sit upright, just so."

She wanted to scream as she watched him remove the belt. He knelt behind her and slid it around her waist. She felt him tug at the strap, and her spine jammed against the tree trunk.

"There, I think that is sufficient for now. Now that I have rested, I must leave you for a short while. I regret that I must close your mouth. You understand?"

She nodded slowly.

He pulled a sweaty rag that might have been a handkerchief from around his neck and rolled it into a strip. "Pardon. It is necessary while I go to fetch our transportation. You will be able to breathe, I promise."

She choked as he tied the cloth around her face.

"Sleep, *ma belle*. When I return, we shall have a long ride before us."

He walked away.

Amy sat still, her heart thumping. He had left her alone, after all. *Thank You, God! Thank You.*

She wriggled against the tree. The belt cut into her abdomen, but she thought she could stand it. She worked her wrists, trying to get hold of the cord that held them. If only she could reach the end, but the thong was tight. Her head throbbed on the left side, and her cheek stung where he had hit her. She leaned back against the tree trunk.

She could hear LeBeau's footsteps, cautious in the brush. He was going after horses, he'd said. Where was his friend?

Her head hurt, and she slumped against the tree trunk, her eyes closed. It came over her very slowly that her protector was gone.

Tom!

She cried bitterly but silently. The last thing she wanted was for LeBeau or his friend to hear her. She drew her knees up and muffled her face in the fold of the dirty skirt.

As the moon rose high above, she turned to God in her silent anguish. *You're all I have, Lord. Tom is gone, and I have only You to keep me safe. Please do not fail in Your promise.* Her own thoughts startled her, and her tears flowed freely. *Lord, I've counted on Tom's strength more than on Yours! I've been very foolish. Forgive me. Whatever You have planned for me, I'm ready.*

She sat quietly, recognizing God's peace and feeling calm. Her cheek stung. The foul-tasting cloth chafed and hindered her breathing. She rubbed her face against her shoulder, trying to dislodge it, but it was tied too tightly.

Suddenly she sat very still.

I must close your mouth. It is necessary. Why was it necessary? If Tom were dead, who would hear her scream?

A bounding hope lifted her heart. Exhausted as she was, she renewed her struggles.

❧

Longing for daylight, Tom trotted Kip up the hill. He rode along the edge of the scraggly pines, hoping LeBeau had brought Amy up from the deep ravine, but he found no sign of them. After scouting all along the hillside to the edge of the defile, he dismounted and let the reins fall. He wasn't sure how deep Kip's training went, but he knew the big gelding wouldn't stray far. He hated to think LeBeau might take possession of the noble horse and reluctantly left Kip grazing.

Tom went to the place where he had made the descent earlier. There was no campfire to guide him, no sound but the wind. Slowly, he worked his way down to the ledge he had sat on when parlaying with LeBeau.

She can't be far, he thought. He wanted to call her name but couldn't risk revealing his location to LeBeau. *Lord, let me find her alive!*

He jumped down from the ledge and ran toward the thick brush, pushing the branches aside.

Here was the place he had seen LeBeau dragging her. He listened for any telltale sound, but the wind in the pines mocked him. He crept along silent as a cat, growing more desperate. If LeBeau had taken her away and was tracking the horses, he might be throwing away his only chance to rescue Amy. He went on, lifting low branches and peering into the shadows.

He came to the place where LeBeau had fired from the thicket and went forward one muffled step at a time toward the last place he had seen his adversary. It was too dark to look for footprints.

"Amy!" he called in desperation. He heard no answer.

For an hour, he crept about in the ravine. He thrashed through every thicket and scrambled up and down the slopes until he was sure Amy was no longer in the small canyon.

At last he sat down. Pain seared through his shoulder, and

it was hard to think. But he was close to where he'd last seen Amy, and he didn't want to leave the place.

He lowered his head into his hands. *Lord, help me. What do I do? This is beyond me.*

If I were LeBeau, I'd be out there looking for my horse, he decided. No matter what happened tonight, if the Frenchman lived, he would need a mount. But Tom hated to give up his search for Amy.

He decided to go a little farther, toward the gap at the east end of the ravine where he could hear the trickle of a brook. If he didn't find anything there, he would turn back.

The moon was high, what there was of it, but it was very dark in the bottom of the draw. He went slowly, until a faint rustle ahead stopped him.

"Amy?"

A low moan, more desperate than the wind, made him rush forward, still wary.

Suddenly he saw her. She thrashed her feet helplessly. He ran to where she sat against a small tree. Her huge eyes stared at him from above a strip of cloth that was tied around her head, through her mouth.

"Amy, precious Amy!" He fumbled at the strip of cloth that gagged her. Unable to loosen the knot, he pulled his knife from his boot.

"Hold still."

He sliced through the cloth and pulled it from her face. Amy gasped and stared up at him, tears in her eyes.

"Tom!" Her mouth shaped the word soundlessly.

"Where's LeBeau?"

"He went to look for the horses."

Tom could barely hear her. He decided he could risk a light if LeBeau was not close by. He took a match from his pouch and tipped her chin upward before striking the light. A welt swelled below her right eye. Her face was filthy, and a bruise spread along her left cheek from the temple toward the eye and down in front of her ear.

"What hurts?" he asked.

"Everything. I can't. . .breathe."

He looked behind her, then blew out the match. LeBeau had cut Layton's gun belt into strips and tied Amy's ankles with thongs. Her hands were secured behind her, and a stout brown belt tightly circled her waist and the tree trunk. In the darkness, he felt for the end of the belt and pulled it. She gasped as it tightened, then he released her, and she fell forward against him with a groan. He caught her and held her in his arms, shaking, his breath as ragged as hers.

"Amy, hold on. You're going to be all right."

"Tom."

"Yes, sweetheart."

"He told me. . . ." She gulped air and swallowed.

"Let me get you loose."

"My feet are numb."

He sliced the thongs on her wrists, and she brought her hands around to the front with a groan and rubbed her wrists.

"Are you bleeding?"

"I don't think so."

He checked her wrists, feeling the deep creases where the leather had been. She had struggled against them, and that knowledge strengthened the love and sorrow in his heart.

He slid the tip of his knife beneath the leather that bound her ankles.

"Where are your boots?"

She looked to her right. "Over there, I think. He took them away in case I got loose." Her voice was still a croak.

Tom rubbed her ankles without self-consciousness.

"Can you feel that?"

She shook her head. "Oh! Yes! Now I can." She caught her breath. "My feet are prickly."

"I'm sorry. Just relax. The blood's flowing again. It will stop hurting in a minute."

She nodded and bit her bottom lip.

⅋

When the agonizing stabs of pain began to fade, Amy reached down and took over the rubbing. *What would Elaine say?* she wondered. *A man rubbing my feet. That could cause a scandal in Albany.*

Tom got up and searched the brush, returning soon with her boots and hat and the buckle and holster from the gun belt.

"I'm so sorry," she whispered. "I ought to have shot him when he first rode up to me, but I panicked. I forgot I even had the pistol until I'd run partway down here."

He dropped beside her on the ground and took her in his arms.

"It doesn't matter. You're all right now." He pulled her head down on his shoulder and stroked her hair.

She clung to him, letting her hands slide up to his shoulders and around his neck. She never wanted to let go of him again.

Suddenly her fingers felt a stiff, ragged place on his shirt behind his left shoulder, and she felt him flinch. She sat back quickly.

"Tom?"

"It's nothing."

"Let me see."

She clambered to her knees, and he turned slightly. His shirt was caked with dried blood on the left side. She probed gently with one finger where the hole was, and he winced.

"They shot you. I thought you jumped off the horse on purpose."

"No. I was thinking about it, but then I got hit. I'm sorry, Amy."

"Sorry? What for?" She burst into tears, wishing she could control it, but she couldn't.

He held her close again, and she felt him kiss the top of her head.

"Tommy," she gasped.

"Shh."

"No, no. He told me—he told me you were dead."

"Oh, honey, I'm so sorry. He's a liar."

Her breath came in short, jagged gulps. "He said Martin shot you and was watching the horses. They were taking me back to Fort Bridger."

"It was the other way around," Tom said. "I killed Martin. I came down here and tried to talk to LeBeau, but he wouldn't let me near you. I got hold of all the horses, then came back to look for you."

Amy made herself take deeper breaths and pulled away from him so she could see his face in the moonlight. His eyes were full of sorrow. She put her hand to his cheek. "I tried not to believe him. He told me that in the morning he would take me to see where you were lying dead. He was smiling."

Tom sighed and tightened his embrace. They sat like that for a long moment.

"We need to get up out of this hole," Tom whispered when she stopped sobbing. "Do you think you can put your boots on?"

She pulled them on gingerly over her sore ankles, then stood up with his support.

"Did you have anything to eat last night?" he asked.

"No."

Tom smiled. "You're going to be so happy. We've got coffee now and bacon. I can even make you some pancakes if the coyotes haven't found the stuff yet."

"We need to get to Fort Laramie," she protested.

"Aren't you hungry?"

She considered. "I think I'm starving."

"I think you are, too. As soon as we find out where LeBeau got to, we're having a hot breakfast. Come on."

Slowly, they inched up the steep wall of the ravine. Tom hauled her up by the hand, one step at a time, stopping three times to let her rest.

"I can't make it," she panted at the third stop.

"Yes, you can. I'll carry you if I have to."

She started to protest but checked herself. Maybe he really could do that. He'd already done the impossible.

She lay against the slope, holding his hand and gathering strength. Pain sliced through her temples every time she moved her head, and her ankles throbbed.

"Let's pray," she whispered.

Tom squeezed her hand and bowed his head. "Lord, thank You for preserving us and bringing us back together. We need some energy now. Please help us to complete our task. I believe You want us to get to Fort Laramie. Please help us do that. Amen."

She gathered up the remnants of her determination. "All right. Let's try again."

When they gained the crest at last, she stumbled forward into the light of the open hillside, and Tom held her up.

"There's Kip," she breathed. "Good old Kip."

"Watch this." Tom gave a whistle, and the gray came trotting, swinging his head with a whicker.

"You clever horse!" Amy stroked his soft nose as he sniffed at her.

Tom stroked the gelding's flank. "He's sweaty!"

Amy reached out in surprise and felt Kip's hot, wet side.

"How long has he been here?"

"I left him at least two hours ago."

"Do you think something's been chasing him? I heard wolves earlier."

"I heard them, too, but they weren't close. And Kip seems calm now. I'm thinking LeBeau tried to get him."

Amy ran her hand along Kip's neck, under the black mane. "Then Kip outran him and came back here to wait for us."

Tom took the canteen from the saddle and opened it for her. She tipped it up and took a mouthful of water, then stood for a moment tasting it, feeling the cool wetness in her mouth and down her throat. She took another sip.

Tom picked her up and put her gently in the saddle, then walked beside the gray, leading him down the hill toward where he had left the gear.

❧

"LeBeau's been here."

Even in the half-light, a quick survey showed Tom that the saddlebags had been plundered and most of their contents strewed on the ground. He had left no weapons, ammunition, or bridles. He was certain now that LeBeau had tried to catch Kip. If he had succeeded, he would have been well armed and mounted once more. He had Layton's pistol, though. As far as Tom knew, only three of the six chambers had been fired.

He looked up at Amy and weighed their options. It wouldn't be long until sunrise. Her safety was, as always, his first priority.

"I want you to take Kip and head for Fort Laramie."

"No."

"Look, LeBeau is ahead of us. He couldn't catch Kip, but he's probably tracking down the other horses."

"I'm not leaving you, Tom."

He sighed. He recognized that stubborn note and knew he'd be wasting time if he argued with her.

"Stay here with Kip, then. And stay mounted. If LeBeau shows up, you skedaddle." She said nothing, and he stared up at her in exasperation. "Amy?"

"All right." Her grudging agreement made him smile.

"Good. LeBeau doesn't have a bridle, and the three saddles are all here, including yours. So if he does manage to come back here with a horse, looking for the tack, you should be able to outrun him." He pulled his pistol from the holster and held it up to her, butt first. "Just in case."

She shook her head. "I let him get the other one from me. You'd better keep it."

"All right, but you've still got the rifle in the scabbard. Now, promise me you'll get out of here if he shows his face."

She hesitated only an instant this time. "I will. Can I switch the saddles?"

"Better wait. I don't want to take a chance on him surprising you while you're on the ground, and if I take time to do it now, I might lose him."

She nodded. "Be careful, Tom."

He holstered the pistol and reached up to squeeze her hand, then turned and ran toward the river, carrying the second musket. He stayed away from the bank, running hard upstream. Banking on LeBeau's moving slowly to track the horses in the scant moonlight, he hurried beyond the watering place, running as fast as he could. His pounding footsteps seemed loud as thunder, but he trusted the flowing river to hide the sound from his enemy.

He swerved toward the bank when he judged he was near the place where he had left the three trappers' horses and peered cautiously over the edge. The pinto was picketed almost directly beneath him. The two hobbled horses had worked their way a few yards upstream but were grazing peacefully. There was no sign of LeBeau. Maybe he was wrong. Tom thought quickly over what he had seen at the pile of gear and concluded again that LeBeau was headed here.

He slid down the steep, six-foot slope, holding the musket pointed skyward. The pinto snorted and lurched away from him, to the end of his tether. The other two horses turned to look at him, still chewing.

Tom flattened himself against the bank and waited. A few minutes later, LeBeau rounded a bend and came toward him, the sound of his steps lost in the river's purling. Tom waited until the man was close to the pinto and had drawn his knife to cut the picket line.

"Hold it right there, LeBeau."

The Frenchman stiffened, then shrugged.

"You cannot blame me for trying, monsieur."

"Drop the knife."

The blade fell to the turf near the picket pin.

"Put your hands up."

LeBeau obeyed, moving with stiff slowness. "Let us be reasonable, my friend."

"And what would you call reasonable?"

"I will tell you where the young lady is."

Tom bit back his reply. If he let slip that he had found Amy and she was within easy reach, his enemy would surely try to overpower him.

"In exchange for one horse," LeBeau added. "You can go get her while I make my way west."

"You'd call that a fair exchange?"

"A generous one. It is to your advantage to find her quickly, you see. Without immediate care, I cannot guarantee she will survive her wounds."

"Her wounds?"

LeBeau spread his hands. "What can I say? She was not cooperative." He took a step toward Tom.

"Don't come any closer."

"You are her personal guard, is it not so? You have a promise to keep. She needs you." He took another step.

"Hold it, or I'll drop you right there," Tom growled.

"No, you will not."

"I will." Tom swallowed. He was tempted to just shoot the man and be done with it. He didn't relish the thought of escorting LeBeau all the way to Fort Laramie. No one would know if he executed him here and now and saved the army the trouble.

He thrust the thought out of his mind and concentrated on the immediate danger. LeBeau must still have Layton's pistol. Tom had to disarm him. As long as he was free and had a weapon, LeBeau would try to make Amy his prisoner again. Tom was determined not to let Amy spend another minute under LeBeau's control, no matter what the cost.

He brandished the musket. "Lie down, LeBeau."

"Monsieur?" The Frenchman's eyebrows arched in shock. "What is this?"

"Do you think I'm an idiot? Lie down now."

LeBeau stared at him for a moment, then slowly lowered his hands, leaning forward. Tom's trigger finger twitched. He expected the man to make a move.

Don't wait, he told himself. *That's what Amy did. She waited too long. He'll shoot you and take her away.*

LeBeau didn't know Amy had been found, Tom reminded himself. He would play his last card to get the horses, then go back for his hostage. He would find her near the saddles, and he would not give her up again. The thought sickened Tom and made his heart race.

LeBeau whistled suddenly, and behind Tom the horses moved restlessly.

"Get down!" Tom shouted.

He was startled as the brown gelding inched up even with him, snuffling. The horse was out of his reach, several paces toward the river but only twenty yards from LeBeau. Even though the brown was hobbled, he was slowly moving toward his master.

It's now or never, Tom thought. *If I don't do something, his horse will get to him.* Even as his gaze wavered between the Frenchman and the gelding, LeBeau's hand went behind him.

fourteen

Amy waited, shivering, on Kip's back. As the minutes stretched toward daybreak, she struggled to conquer her dread.

Lord, she prayed, *I know You can help us. Forgive me for trusting Tom more than I trusted You. And if there's anything I can do to help him now, please show me.*

Her bruised cheek throbbed as she brushed a tear away.

Kip tugged at the reins, and she thought he wanted to graze, but when she slackened her hold, he began walking toward the river.

"All right, boy," Amy whispered. "I'm with you. You know where they are." She glanced up toward the velvet sky. *Lord, I told him we'd run if LeBeau came, but even Kip doesn't want to stay here alone. Please, help me not to do anything stupid.*

The gray lengthened his stride and ran swiftly up the riverbank, not checking until they were above where the Frenchman stood, facing Tom. LeBeau's back was to Amy, and in the first ray of dawn, she caught the gleam of gunmetal where the pistol was tucked in the back of his waistband. In an instant, she took in Tom's wary stance, his musket pointed at LeBeau's chest, and with horror she saw that the brown horse was working his way toward LeBeau. In another moment, he would shield the trapper from Tom.

❧

As Tom made his choice, he heard drumming hoofbeats above him, and he saw LeBeau whip the pistol from behind his back. The Frenchman leveled the Colt, and in the instant when Tom would have squeezed the trigger of his musket, a huge body flew off the bank above. As Kip slammed into LeBeau, the pistol discharged in the air. The horses squealed and scattered, and LeBeau sprawled on the ground.

Kip landed hard in the soft earth by the water and stumbled into the shallows. Amy looked tiny on the big gray's back, and she fell heavily forward on impact, flying up toward Kip's ears. She clung tenaciously to the gray's neck, struggling to regain her balance and push herself back into the saddle.

Tom forced his attention back to LeBeau. The leaping horse had knocked him down, but he had rolled with the impact and was crouching, breathing hard and cocking the revolver. He was aiming not at Tom but at Amy.

Tom drew a quick bead on LeBeau's chest, steady and accurate, and the musket roared. LeBeau stood stock still for an instant, seeming undecided whether to fall or not. Then he tumbled back and lay still.

Tom put one shaking hand to his face and swallowed hard.

The pinto crow-hopped nervously, but the picket rope held him. Kip floundered out of the water and stood trembling, with Amy, wide-eyed, staring down from his back at Tom. The brown horse edged away from Kip and put his head down to crop the grass. He was calm now, eating without concern for his former owner.

Tom laid down his musket and walked slowly toward LeBeau, pulling his revolver.

The Frenchman's eyes were open, staring sightlessly at the sky. Tom kicked his boot gently. He stooped and retrieved Layton's pistol, tucking it in his belt, then let the hammer of his own gun down carefully and holstered it.

He turned toward Amy. She held her arms out toward him, and he stepped to Kip's side and lifted her from the saddle.

She took a deep breath, her lips quivering. "I'm sorry, Tom. I couldn't stand being alone, not knowing, and Kip wanted to come, too."

He pulled her close and stroked her shimmering hair. She was shivering. He wanted to scold her, to let loose all the things his father would have yelled at him. *You could have broken your neck. You could have been shot. You might have gotten us both killed.*

He couldn't say any of those things. "Shh. It's all right. Things might have gone differently if you hadn't come. I wasn't thinking very clearly."

He felt her small hands slip around him, and he let himself hold her a few more seconds before ruefully pushing her away. "Come on. Let's see if Kip is all right."

Her eyes widened then, vivid blue in the early light. She turned quickly to the horse, anxiously running her hands along his forelegs, her delicate fingers probing gently.

"Poor Kip," she crooned.

Tom took the reins and urged the gray to walk slowly down the grassy strip. "Is he limping?"

"No, he's fine. But, Tom, everything my father ever said about me is true. I'm reckless and foolhardy. I promised him I'd keep Kip safe, but when I thought LeBeau was going to kill you, I forgot all that!"

Tom looked down at his dusty boots. "I made a promise to the major, too."

Pain flooded her face. "What do we do now?"

"Can you tie the horses together? I'll take care of LeBeau."

He carried the body away from the water and forced himself to go through LeBeau's pockets. He found only a few coins and a folding knife. Around the man's neck was a cord that held half a dozen bear claws and a crucifix. He thought fleetingly of salvaging it for LeBeau's brother. But if justice were served, Raymond LeBeau would be hanged for horse stealing. To whom would the major send his personal effects? Tom left the necklace.

When he straightened, Amy stood a few feet away, holding Kip's reins and the end of the picket rope. Tom took the rope from her. "You take Kip up the bank, and I'll bring the other horses."

A buzzard rose as they approached the pile of saddles and gear. It flapped south toward the hills. Amy gasped.

Tom said grimly, "I'm sorry. I ought to bury Martin and LeBeau before we leave."

She closed her eyes, then opened them again. "We don't have a shovel, and we can't afford to stop that long."

Tom mulled over her words for a moment, then nodded. "I'm really sorry. I shouldn't have left him here. All I could think about was finding you."

She dismounted and dropped Kip's reins, coming close to touch her fingers to his cheek. "I'm glad you did. For a while I was hopeful, but then I gave up. I thought I heard your voice in the night, and I told myself it was just the wind. When I saw you, I still couldn't believe it was you. I thought I was going crazy."

He swallowed hard. "Sit down over there, Amy. I'll fix you something to eat. No arguments."

He quickly gathered fuel for a fire and picked up a tinderbox from the scattered stuff on the ground. The pain in his shoulder stabbed deep, and he hoped the bleeding wouldn't start again. In a few minutes, he had a small blaze going and had put some bacon in a pan over the flames. Amy watched as he brought the dented little coffeepot over and poured water from one of the outlaws' canteens into it.

"I can make the coffee."

"All right." He looked hard at her and decided she was over the shock. "I've got to do a few things."

She nodded.

He walked slowly toward where Martin lay. He hated to leave the bodies exposed, but Amy was right; they had little choice. Without digging tools, he couldn't bury them deep enough to keep the wolves from unearthing them.

He braced himself and stared down at Martin's ghastly corpse, then turned quickly away. He'd tell the colonel where the bodies were, but he doubted there would be anything left when the colonel's men arrived.

He walked slowly back to where Amy sat. She threw worried

glances toward him as he approached.

"I found the flour and baking powder. I'm making griddle cakes."

Tom nodded, not sure he could eat any. He sat down on the grass a few feet from her.

"Tom. . ." She pressed her lips together and poured batter into the frying pan.

He sat without speaking until she brought him two griddle cakes and a slab of bacon on a tin plate, along with a cup of steaming coffee.

"Thanks. I ought to be waiting on you."

"Tom, you did what you had to, and I'm very thankful."

Her eyes were sober. When he looked at her bruised face, he was still angry.

"If I just could have gotten to you sooner," he began.

She shook her head. "I'll be fine, Tom. You had to deal with other things. It's over now."

He set the plate down and held out his arms. She came to him, and he squeezed her, just tight enough to assure himself she was real and she was safe. Tears trickled down his face.

"Amy, I'm sorry I wasn't there when he hurt you."

"You keep saying that, but you've got to stop. We don't need to think about last night."

"I can't help thinking about it. I felt so helpless while you were with him."

She was silent, but her hands softly rubbed his back.

He remembered her hasty declaration of love before he'd fallen from Kip's back the day before. Did she really love him, even now? He had bungled her rescue badly, allowing the loathsome LeBeau to detain her for several hours. He ought to have been able to avoid that somehow. He ought to have immediately faced down the Frenchman, not let him drag her through the woods and inflict untold misery on her.

"He hit you, didn't he?"

She took two deep breaths before she answered. "Let's not

tell Father about this, Tom."

He leaned back to look at her. "I have to report to the major, Amy. We can't just pretend none of this happened."

She sighed. "All right, but please, Tom, don't tell him that. . ." She buried her face in his shoulder, and he held her, shuddering. It was worse than he'd thought.

"I knew I shouldn't have waited," he choked.

She touched his cheek and wiped away a tear.

"The filthy swine—"

"Stop it." She was stern, and he held his tongue.

"Eat," he said at last, picking up the plate and holding it out to her.

"That's for you."

"I'm not hungry."

"Yes, you are."

"No." He glanced involuntarily toward the place where he'd left the outlaw's body. "I really don't think I can."

A frown came over Amy's face. "The first chance I get to cook for you, and you won't eat."

He shook his head, unable to keep from smiling. "All right, but you've got to eat, too."

She went back to the fire and dribbled more batter into the frying pan.

Tom picked up a pancake and bit into it, forcing himself not to think about Martin's face. "This is good." He picked up the cooling cup of coffee and took a swallow.

"Which horse do I ride?" Amy asked.

"Kip, of course, unless you want to give him a rest. But he's recovered, I think."

She smiled. "And which one are you taking?"

"The bay. If you want, we can turn the others loose."

"Don't be silly. We need to take them all back to Fort Laramie. You ought to be able to have them. You need to replace Buck and. . ." She faltered. "I mean, you saved my life."

He laughed shortly. "Well, you saved mine, too."

He got up to saddle the horses. Amy brought him the saddlebags, and he tied the rope between the pinto and the brown gelding so he could lead them both.

"All set?"

"I found this," Amy said hesitantly. She held up a dusty hat. "You lost yours, and you really need one."

He stared at it for a moment, then reached out and took it. Slowly, he settled it on his head.

"Let's go." He put his foot in the stirrup of the bay's saddle.

❧

Amy felt a little uncertain, let down somehow. Things had changed. Tom's tenderness was gone. It was more like the first night they'd ridden together from Fort Bridger, when he had let her do everything for herself and kept his distance. For an instant, she wished they were both riding Kip again, with Tom sitting behind her with his arms around her.

They picked their way up the long hill and over the crest. The terrain was rugged, and in a narrow spot, he held back and let her go first. Amy couldn't see him then, but she thought he was brooding, dreading the moment when he would tell her father all that had happened. He had held her in his arms that morning, giving her immense comfort, but apparently it wasn't enough for him.

Perhaps he thought the major would be angry because of her close call. He was probably thinking about Layton and Brown as well. He'd lost two men and almost forfeited her life and his own. She knew Tom felt he hadn't come off very well and that he wouldn't try to make himself look good. She wanted to make him see somehow that he had no cause for guilt.

If Tom could understand how lonely and forsaken she had felt in the darkness of the night when LeBeau told her so blithely that he was dead! She wanted him to know the palpable, bubbling joy she'd experienced when he had come to release her. God had answered her prayer in a way she hadn't thought possible. Her bitter grief had been banished in an instant. She could deal with the rest: the pain, the terror, the hopelessness. She would not forget, but she would heal.

She was not so sure about Tom. He was quiet and had distanced himself from her, physically and emotionally. He had said nothing of love, only of guilt and sorrow.

When they got to the fort, he would probably be glad to have his troublesome charge off his hands. It was a bleak prospect for Amy.

fifteen

For two hours they rode in silence, letting the horses pick the easiest path over the hills, then they moved back toward the Platte. They came to the last ford, where a ferry was tied. The wagon road came up out of the river and climbed the bluffs on the south bank, running high above the water toward Fort Laramie. Despite the pain in his shoulder, Tom felt a surge of relief. They were really going to make it.

Amy jumped down and let Kip wade into the water, holding his reins as he drank. Tom brought the other three horses to the water's edge and sloshed into the water, trying to hold them all steady. The pinto pulled at the rope, and it sent a sharp pain through his shoulder.

"We're nearly there," said Amy.

"Twenty miles."

"Should we let them rest?"

"For a few minutes."

When the horses finished drinking, he led them away from the river's edge. He dropped the bay's reins and let him graze near Kip, but he didn't trust the other two, particularly the pinto. He held the lead rope and stood near them, taking a step or two when they moved to new grass. Amy stayed near Kip, a few yards away.

Tom's eyes kept straying to where she stood, small and forlorn. He thought about moving nearer to her so they could talk, but it seemed too much trouble. He was tired, very tired, and his shoulder ached. His head ached, too. He sat down and drew his knees up, leaning his head on them. When the rope stretched taut, he yanked it with his right hand, but the pinto kept tugging insistently. He got slowly to his feet and moved a few paces.

Finally he decided they had stopped long enough and pulled the two horses toward Amy.

"Best go on," he said.

She nodded and pulled Kip's head up.

She was crying, the tears flowing unrestrained down her cheeks.

He turned and put his arms over the pinto's saddle and leaned on the horse. He ought to be able to keep her from crying. It cut deep that he had won her back from the Frenchman and she was still weeping. His fists clenched. Why had he hesitated to shoot LeBeau? He ought to have dropped him the second he appeared.

"Tom."

He turned to face Amy. She had come softly and stood beside him now.

"Are you all right?" she asked, her brow furrowed.

She had not wiped the tears away. He wondered if she knew she was crying. The feelings inside him roiled. He looked away toward the river and took a deep breath.

"I'll be fine."

"Maybe we should do something to that wound."

He shook his head. "Nothing but dirty water here. Maybe I'll have the surgeon look at it when we get to the fort."

"You'd better."

He took another breath.

"Tom, are you all right?"

"I just told you—"

"It's more than the wound, isn't it?"

He tried to avoid her tender gaze, but his eyes were drawn back to her. "Amy, I never killed a man before. Until yesterday, I mean."

She nodded, her blue eyes solemn.

"That first one," he said, "the big man. . .Oliver. He was so far away, it didn't seem so bad. But Martin. . ." He swallowed.

Amy's touch was delicate on his sleeve. "You had to, Tom. It was him or you. I know that. God knows, too."

He turned away. He had seen men shot before, had seen them die. But the horror of seeing the man's face when the bullet struck was still vivid.

"I know I had to, but it was so. . ." He let his thoughts trail off. "And LeBeau this morning." He shook his head. "He saw I was weak. I almost couldn't pull the trigger. Even though I knew he was a cold-blooded murderer—Amy, he was going to kill me, and I still didn't want to do it."

"You think that's bad? Tom, it's a serious thing to take a life."

"But I knew what he was. I'd seen what he did to you, and I still couldn't shoot him until he went after you again."

"Tom." She pulled him around gently to face her. "You didn't fail. When the moment came, you didn't fail. If he'd drawn on you, you would have fired, just like with the others. Call it duty or self-defense or whatever you like."

He sighed, and she reached tentatively toward his face. He wasn't sure he wanted her to touch him. He felt unworthy. He might have kept her alive, but he had still failed the test. He hadn't kept her safe. That was part of the major's commission. Alive and safe were two different things.

"Tom, you're burning up!"

His eyes were dull, and he seemed to have trouble focusing on her. Amy pressed her hand to his forehead, below the hat brim.

"You have a fever."

"I'm all right."

"No, you're not."

She opened a saddlebag and came up with a dirty piece of cloth. She walked rapidly to the brink of the stream and dipped the cloth in it.

"Here, take your hat off.

He looked at her apathetically. She pulled the hat from his head and sponged his brow with the rag.

"Come on. We need to get you to the fort."

She almost pushed him up onto the bay's back, and she took the lead rope herself.

"Can you sit a trot?"

"Of course I can."

She smiled grimly. He was well enough to let his pride flare up.

"Hang on. If you fall off that horse, I won't be able to get you back on him."

"I told you, I'm all right."

She was torn between making the horses walk gently to spare him pain and getting him to the fort as fast as possible.

They trotted on at a good pace for half an hour. The pinto repeatedly sidled up to Kip and nipped at his flanks. When he nuzzled at Amy's leg and bared his teeth, she slapped him hard on the nose.

"Get out of here, you mangy crow bait!" She wished Tom had tied him on the other side of the brown.

Up ahead, she saw a small tuft of dust. She pulled Kip to a halt, and Tom's horse stopped beside them.

"What is it?" he asked.

"Someone's ahead of us."

Tom stood in his stirrups, staring down the trail. "Going toward the fort."

"Yes."

"Come on." He urged the bay forward, and she followed, pulling the stubborn pinto and the brown horse along.

Tom's bay began to canter, and Amy struggled to keep the three horses under control.

She heard a whoop from Tom, but the dust was flying. She couldn't see the cause of his animation until Kip was nearly on the bay's tail.

Tom leaped to the ground beside a chestnut horse.

"Well, T.R., what do you know!" the man leading the horse cried.

"Private Brown!" Amy wrapped the lead rope around the saddle horn and slid to the ground.

"Well, Miss Travis! You look a bit worse for wear. What happened?"

She laughed. "Private Brown, you're a sight for sore eyes. Tom's been shot, and I've been doing my best to get him to the post surgeon at Laramie."

"Shot?" Brown turned to Tom in surprise. "Can't be too bad."

"Got a piece of lead in my shoulder." Tom shrugged.

"You make it sound like nothing," Amy scolded.

Brown looked at her keenly. "What happened to the riders?"

"Dead," said Tom.

Brown nodded. "Good for you. I thought sure they had you two."

"Your horse is lame," Amy observed. Lady was holding one hind foot off the ground.

"Yes, she threw a shoe on the other side of the Platte. I've been walking all morning."

Tom laughed. "Pick a horse from Amy's string."

Brown grinned. "Sounds good to me." He turned and surveyed the horses, then looked quickly at Tom. "Where's old Buck?"

"Shot out from under me," Tom said glumly.

"Too bad." Brown eyed the pinto speculatively. "How does that spotted horse handle?"

Tom grimaced. "He's pretty and he's fast, but he's got no manners."

"I knew a girl like that once," Brown said thoughtfully.

Tom chuckled, and Amy blushed.

"Guess I'll give him a tryout." The trooper untied the lead rope.

Amy watched Tom anxiously as he put his foot in the stirrup. He started to mount, then settled back on the ground. She took a step toward him, but he was trying again, and this time he heaved himself into the saddle.

She said nothing and mounted Kip. Brown insisted on leading Lady and the dark brown gelding, and they proceeded at a walk to accommodate the mare.

"How did you get away from the riders?" Amy asked. "We saw them chase you across the ford there by Independence Rock."

"Yes, it went just the way I planned it, except they were closer than I liked. I think it wasn't long before they realized you weren't ahead of me. Maybe it was the tracks or just the fact that there wasn't enough dust flying; I don't know. Anyway, Lady gave it her best, and we started to lengthen our lead. After ten miles or so, she was about winded, and I realized all of a sudden that they weren't back there anymore."

"What did you do?" Amy glanced at Tom. He was slouched in the saddle, and she wondered how alert he was.

"Well, I had to let Lady rest awhile. I thought about back-tracking and following them, but I figured at the next ford I'd cross the river again, and we could meet up. Except when I crossed, I couldn't tell if you'd passed already, then it commenced to rain. Say, did you two get wet that night?"

"Did we ever!" Amy cried. "The lightning drove Kip wild."

"We holed up in old Jim Frye's cabin," Tom said. "You know the place?"

"I heard there was a house along there someplace, but I never saw it. Too bad I couldn't have found you."

Amy laughed. "I don't think another horse could have fit in that cabin."

"You took the horses inside?" Brown laughed.

"Made it nice and cozy," said Tom.

Brown sighed with envy. "That was the most miserable night I've ever spent. Lady and I snuggled down in a dip and liked to have froze."

As they went on, Amy kept an anxious eye on Tom.

"So, Miss Travis, you took a tumble?" Brown was looking at her face, and Amy realized she must be quite a sight.

"Yes, I–I fell from a rock, then. . ." She stopped and glanced toward Tom, but he was silent, his eyes nearly closed.

Brown said quietly, "I hope you weren't too badly hurt."

"No, it's nothing, really."

Brown nodded.

They went on in silence until Tom slumped low in his saddle. Amy pushed Kip up beside the bay. "Tom, are you all right? Hold on!"

"Here, Miss Travis, take this."

Brown was beside her, handing her the lead rope. He maneuvered the pinto to Tom's other side and grasped his arm.

"You're going to make it, T.R. Just look up ahead, fella. I can see the top of the west watchtower."

Tom stirred. "Hurts bad, Mike."

"I know. Come on, now, nice and easy." Brown leaned over and took the reins gently from Tom's hand.

Amy dropped back a bit and followed with the lead line, renewing her prayers. Brown kept one hand on Tom's shoulder. They passed the large Sioux village outside the fort complex and approached the gate. Brown hailed the first soldier he saw.

"Tell Colonel Munroe we have urgent news from Fort Bridger, and ask for the surgeon!"

They went on, past the trading post, blacksmith shop, and barracks, toward the commander's quarters.

"T.R.?" A young trooper detached himself from a cluster of men and came quickly toward them.

"You're Matthew," Brown said.

"Yes, I'm his brother. What happened?" The young man looked from Brown to Amy and back to the inert Tom.

"He got shot yesterday. Help me get him to the surgeon." Brown leaned toward Tom. "Come on, fella. We're here."

Tom opened one eye.

"Just lean on me, and we'll help you down. Got to get you to the doc."

"You're not going to carry me in," Tom protested weakly,

then slid over the side to the ground in a heap.

Brown looked at Matt Barkley.

"Sorry, son. At least we got him here." He dismounted, handing his reins to one of the troopers who had gathered.

A corporal bustling with importance approached him. "Private, you're in from Fort Bridger?"

"Yes, I'm Michael Brown. This man is T. R. Barkley, and we have dispatches for Colonel Munroe." He gestured toward Amy. "The young lady is Major Travis's daughter. Could someone offer her hospitality?"

"Of course."

Amy sat on Kip's back with the activity swirling around her. Matt called to two of his friends, and they carried Tom toward the surgeon's office. Brown gave instructions for Lady to be taken to the blacksmith and for the other horses to be fed and turned out.

"I'll take you to Colonel Munroe now," the corporal told him.

"May I take your horse, ma'am?" a freckle-faced young private asked.

"Thank you." Amy climbed down wearily, staggering as she hit the ground.

The corporal said uncertainly, "If you'd like to wait, miss, I can send someone to take you to one of the officers' wives."

Brown roared, "This young lady has come from Fort Bridger in four days and is exhausted. What's more, she needs medical attention. You will not leave her standing on the parade ground."

The corporal trembled, and Amy thought he almost croaked, "Yes, sir!" before he remembered Brown was only a private. He looked sheepishly at Amy. "Would you come this way, miss?"

She followed him and Brown wearily, wishing she had followed Tom instead. Within minutes, Brown was explaining their mission to the colonel and delivering Major Travis's dispatches.

"The scout Barkley believes the situation is urgent, sir."

"Hm, yes." Munroe scanned the papers Brown had handed him. "We sent a small detachment out a few days ago."

"We met them on the Sweetwater Tuesday evening," Brown said quickly. "Seven troopers and a few civilians. We believe three trappers learned Miss Travis was with us and left their camp to follow us. They killed Private Layton at Independence Rock and wounded the scout. Miss Travis has had a very strenuous journey, sir."

The colonel looked sympathetically toward Amy. "I'm distressed that you suffered such an ordeal. My wife will be delighted to have you as a visitor until you have news from your father."

"Thank you," Amy murmured, wondering if the colonel's wife would let her have a bath immediately.

"You say three men followed you back along the Sweetwater to Independence Rock?" Colonel Munroe surveyed the map on the office wall.

"Yes, sir, this is where we met them." Brown stepped forward and pinpointed the location. "It wasn't until the next day that we were aware of the pursuit. Apparently the ringleader, LeBeau, had designs on Miss Travis."

"LeBeau?" Munroe asked. "He left here with the detachment. Major Lynde had received word from Fort Bridger that the man's brother was being detained for horse stealing. I was sending back permission for Major Travis to handle the case as he saw fit, but LeBeau asked if he could go along and perhaps speak up for his brother or at least see him again. I let him go. You say there were others?"

"Yes, a big, bearded man named Oliver, with a flashy paint horse, and a fair, snake-eyed man in buckskins."

"Don't know them," said Munroe, "but I haven't been here long. So they saw Miss Travis and—"

"No, sir, they most certainly did not see her that night," Brown interrupted. "Barkley made sure of that. But he did tell the corporal he was bringing her to Fort Laramie. I suspect that after we left, the corporal let it slip."

Munroe frowned. "Miss Travis, my deepest apologies. I'll look into this matter."

Amy took a deep breath. "LeBeau told me he hoped to trade me for his brother's life at Fort Bridger."

"You spoke to him?" Munroe asked.

"Y—yes. He. . ." She looked at the two men. Brown's face was full of compassion, and Munroe's gaze was riveted on her. "Mr. Barkley and I became separated from Private Brown in an attempt to outwit them. Mr. Barkley shot the man Oliver, but the other two came after us. They wounded Barkley, and. . ." She gulped. "LeBeau kidnapped me, sir. He held me for several hours and tried to get the horses back from Barkley."

Brown reached over and patted her hand.

There was a knock at the door, and a woman of forty entered the room, her pleasant face drawn into a worried frown.

"Miss Travis?"

"Yes." Amy stood shakily, and the colonel and Brown leaped to their feet.

"My dear, this is Major Travis's daughter. Miss Travis, my wife, Elizabeth."

It was so proper that Amy thought she might laugh, but instead she found to her dismay that she was crying.

Mrs. Munroe stepped quickly toward her, putting an arm around her shoulders.

"Come, dear. You need a rest and a bath and a good meal."

"I should like to write a note to my father," Amy said.

"Of course," the colonel agreed. "My wife will see to it, and I'll send it out."

The last thing Amy heard was Brown saying, "Please have the surgeon look at her, too, ma'am."

Then she collapsed gently against Mrs. Munroe. Brown reached out hastily and caught her before she could sink to the floor.

sixteen

They kept Amy in bed for a day. She protested, but Dr. Johns insisted, and Mrs. Munroe proved to be a fierce watchdog. The first time Amy awakened, her hostess spooned broth into her mouth and urged her to go back to sleep.

"I need to write to Father," Amy said with determination but little stamina.

When Amy had scrawled the note, Mrs. Munroe took it away, leaving her guest to sink back on the soft feather pillow and surrender to fatigue.

It was dark when Amy woke again, and a small lamp flickered at the bedside. A strange woman leaned toward her, saying, "Well, now." She disappeared for a few minutes and came back with a cup of tea well laced with sugar. Amy swallowed most of it, then drifted back into her dreams.

They were not all pleasant dreams. In most of them, she was riding Kip, sometimes pounding across the prairie in an impromptu race with Trooper Brown. At other times, she was frightened, looking constantly over her shoulder as Kip galloped away from some sinister presence. At last she dreamed she was riding along slowly, and Tom was on the horse with her. His arms encircled her, and she leaned her head back against his shoulder. It was so soothing, she wished she could stay in that dream, but then LeBeau came trotting along beside them on the pinto, smiling and calling, *"Réveillez, mademoiselle!"* He pointed a revolver at Tom. *"Pardonez moi,"* he said graciously, "it is the necessity."

She awoke with a start, trembling.

"Good morning," said Mrs. Munroe, laying aside her embroidery hoop. "Do you feel up to having some breakfast, my dear?"

"Tom—" Amy said weakly.

152

"I beg your pardon?"

"Tom—Mr. Barkley. Is he all right? Where is he?"

"Oh, the scout." Mrs. Munroe smiled. "He's still in the infirmary. The report this morning was that he needs rest. His wound was infected, I believe."

Amy struggled to sit up. She was wearing a soft pink nightgown she had never seen before.

"Do you feel well enough to get up, dear? Because I can bring you a tray. Dr. Johns said that you might get up if your head isn't aching too badly."

"I–I want to get up."

"Perhaps you'd like a bath. I washed you up a bit, but travel is so. . .uncomfortable."

Amy grimaced, remembering her state when she had arrived at the fort. "I'd love a bath."

It was not until late in the afternoon that she was able to convince her hostess that she was up to visiting the infirmary. Private Brown, who had stopped to inquire about Amy, took her part and offered to escort her, so Mrs. Munroe let her go.

"Don't worry, ma'am, I'll bring her back shortly," Brown said.

"Thank you," Amy breathed when Mrs. Munroe closed her door. "I was feeling a bit smothered."

"You look charming."

She looked down at her borrowed dress. "Every stitch I have on except my boots belongs to someone else."

"It suits you."

"Thank you. Has the colonel sent relief to my father?"

"Yes, forty men. They left at dawn."

"You didn't go with them?"

"Colonel Munroe asked me to stay to help with some details since T.R. hasn't been able to brief him yet."

"Tom is very ill?" she asked anxiously.

Brown shrugged. "He's tough. They removed the bullet first thing."

He opened the door to the surgery, and she stepped in out of the baking sun.

Tom lay very still on a cot. His shoulder was bandaged, and a blanket covered him to his chest, despite the warmth of the day. His breathing seemed rapid and shallow to Amy, and when she touched his hand, its heat shocked her.

"Has he been awake?" Brown asked.

The infirmary aide shook his head. "Not while I've been here." He wrung out a wet cloth and folded it on Tom's forehead. "We're just trying to keep the fever down."

Brown touched Amy's arm. "Best to let him rest, Miss Travis."

"I want to stay."

"You're hardly well yourself."

She knew it was true. Her head still ached, and her cheek smarted. She had seen her reflection in Mrs. Munroe's mirror after her bath that morning, and the purple bruises frightened her. Her hostess had been generous with gentle soaps and emollients and had offered to help her cover the worst of the bruises with powder.

She touched Tom's cheek with her fingertips. The dark whiskers on his jaw were almost long enough to make a beard now.

"I'll bring you back tomorrow," Brown promised. "I don't think you're ready to sit with him."

Reluctantly, she let the private lead her outside.

&

Tom opened his eyes and lay still, trying to orient himself. He was indoors but not at his house. Not Jim Frye's cabin. He turned his head and saw a shelf of bottles and instruments.

A man in uniform came to the bedside.

"Well, Barkley, how do you feel?"

He swallowed. "Dry."

The man brought him a glass of water. "Easy now. I'll help you sit up a bit."

The effort sent pain ripping through his left shoulder, and sweat broke out on his brow.

"Where am I?" Tom asked as he sank back onto the pillow.

"Fort Laramie. I'm Dr. Johns."

"We made it."

"You certainly did. I've heard part of the story, and I'd say you are a lucky man."

"Is Miss Travis all right?"

"I think so. Concussed and some bruises on her face and arms, one laceration. But I'd say there's nothing serious. She's been in to see you."

The door opened and another man looked in. "Private Brown is here again," he announced.

"He can come in," said the surgeon.

"Mike!"

"Hey, T.R. You look better!" Brown grasped his hand, and Tom winced. "Sorry."

"I'll send some breakfast in for you, Mr. Barkley," the doctor said. "Some oatmeal, I think, and tea."

"Make it coffee," said Tom.

"You *are* feeling better." Johns went out the door.

"Sit down," Tom told Brown eagerly.

"Fever gone?"

"Don't ask me. How long have I been here?"

"Three days."

"Three—are you serious?" Tom asked.

"Yup. The doc operated on you first thing Friday. Today's Monday."

"The dispatches—"

"All taken care of. Munroe sent forty men out Saturday morning. Your brother went with them."

"Matthew!" Tom was startled. His little brother was off to fight Indians, and Tom hadn't even seen him.

"He wanted to go," Brown said.

"He would."

"Well, that's a kid for you."

Tom nodded. He felt old. He had killed three men. Matt had no idea what he was asking for. To him, war was an adventure. Tom thought he had had enough adventure to last a lifetime.

"How's Amy?" He said it offhandedly, without looking at Brown.

"She's fine. Pesters me all the time to bring her over here."

"She came, the doc said."

"Five times so far."

Tom wasn't sure he liked that. "They carried me in here, didn't they?"

"Had to, T.R. I'm sorry."

He nodded grimly. "Well, she's seen me at my worst."

"She sets a lot of store by you."

Tom only grunted.

"What?"

"What am I going to tell Major Travis?"

Brown shrugged. "Colonel Munroe was sympathetic, seemed to think we acted properly, did all we could to complete the mission."

Tom looked up at the ceiling. "He's not her father."

"Still, he outranks Travis, and he sent him word we got through and his daughter was safe. Grilled me pretty hard about Independence Rock and Layton, but overall, I'd say we came off pretty good, T.R."

Tom frowned. "They're not going to give you any grief about Layton, are they? Because if it's anyone's fault, it's mine. I shouldn't have let him go out in front like that and sit there like a stupid target."

"Take it easy. It's nobody's fault he got himself killed. You see three whites riding up on you—you don't expect them to open fire. Don't blame yourself, T.R. We made it. Layton didn't. That's all."

Tom stared toward the window. He couldn't see much from where he lay, only a patch of sky and the corner of the bar-racks roof.

"You did the job," Brown insisted.

"I didn't keep her safe."

Brown stirred. "She seems all right now. I heard what she told the colonel."

"What was that?"

"LeBeau got hold of her and held her a few hours. That's about it. She didn't go into detail."

"Then she just smiled and walked away?"

"No," Brown said uneasily. "Then she. . .well, she was very tired, T.R. But she's fine now. At least, I think she is. She's worried about you, but—"

Tom pounded the mattress with his right fist and turned his head away.

"What really happened?" Brown asked.

"I wish I knew."

Brown said slowly, "Maybe it's better this way."

"Her father's going to kill me."

"Whatever for? You brought her back."

Tom faced him angrily. "I should have walked right up to that. . .that. . ." He laid back in exasperation. There was no word bad enough for LeBeau. "I was afraid I'd hit Amy if I shot at him. He had her down in a little canyon. I was within ten yards of him, but he had Amy. I'm glad she was unconscious. She didn't see me walk away."

"Sounds to me like you didn't have much choice."

"Of course I did. I should have just marched up to him anyway and shot him right between those beady little eyes."

"He'd have killed you before you ever got near him."

"So what? Would that be worse than leaving her with him? Six hours, I make it, Mike! I went and rounded up all the horses. It was the only way I could think of to make sure he couldn't leave with her."

"Seems like a reasonable plan to me, and it worked."

Tom shook his head. "It's what did or did not happen between sunset and moonrise that's bothering me, Mike. I should have faced him down right there in the canyon. Killed him or made him kill me. Hauled her out of there or died trying."

"Listen to you." Brown's eyes were troubled. "You really think it would be better for him to kill you and make off with her than what you did?"

Tom sighed. "If you had been there, you wouldn't have waited."

Brown considered. "I can't say what I would have done. I probably never would have thought to get a corner on the horses. Maybe I would have gone down that canyon blazing. I don't know. Wasted all my ammunition, probably. Then what? I'd be dead, and LeBeau would be dragging Miss Travis off to Bridger."

Tom put his fist to his forehead.

"You don't really think—" Brown looked at him closely, then asked softly, "Was she crying when you found her?"

"Yes. She cried a lot that morning. But once we got on the trail, she seemed better. I don't know. We stopped for water, and she was crying again."

Brown sat back. "Well, T.R., I don't know what to tell you. Just be up front with the major. If there's anything more to reveal, she'll tell him."

Tom bit his lip. "What would you do if it was your wife?"

"Well, I guess. . .I'd ask her. But that's not something you can just ask a single gal. Dr. Johns saw her, though."

Tom nodded. "Bruises, he told me. Cracked her head and had bruises."

"The major's not going to hold you accountable for her injuries."

"Why shouldn't he? Mike, when I saw her at dusk, she didn't have that cut on her right cheek. LeBeau did that to her."

They sat in silence.

The surgeon's aide came in with a tray. "Breakfast, Mr. Barkley."

Tom stared glumly at the tray.

"She'll be wanting to come see you." Brown stood up.

"I don't know, Mike."

"You can't refuse to see her. She's been after me constantly to tell her when you woke up."

"Dr. Johns would like him to rest after he eats," the aide said.

"This afternoon," Brown said, backing toward the door.

❧

Amy stepped cautiously into the infirmary.

"Tom?"

He sat reclining on pillows, a clean shirt pulled over the white bandages on his shoulder, and he had been shaved. He looked younger, she thought at first, but she changed her mind when his dark, brooding eyes met her look.

He didn't speak as she walked to the bedside.

"How do you feel?" she asked to break the silence.

"Awful. But I'll probably be out of here tomorrow."

"Your brother went to Fort Bridger."

"Mike told me."

"I'm sorry you didn't get to see him first. He was very concerned about you."

Tom nodded.

Amy pulled the one straight chair in the room over and perched on the edge of it. "I've been praying so hard that you'd recover. You gave us all a scare."

He said nothing.

"Tom, I want to thank you for—"

"No need," he said curtly.

She paused, a little hurt. He wouldn't look at her.

"Colonel Munroe says we ought to have some news by the end of the week. Captain Hollis is under orders to send word as soon as possible about conditions at Fort Bridger."

Tom nodded again.

"Will you stay until we hear something, Tom?"

"I ought to get back." He turned slowly to look at her. She knew the bruises had faded and the red welt on her cheek was nearly gone, but Tom did not seem pleased with what he saw.

He frowned. "You all right?"

"Yes. I'm fine."

He nodded.

"Tom, you won't. . .just leave. . .without telling me?"

"I'll let you know."

"Thank you. I'm at Colonel Munroe's."

Amy stood up. She smiled tremulously. "I'm glad you're better."

He gave a brief nod, and she slipped out of the room, defeated and heartsick. She stood still outside the door for a moment, then turned to Brown.

"How's the patient?" Brown asked heartily.

She hesitated. "I'm not sure."

"I'll walk you back to the colonel's."

❧

Tom had had enough. He'd moved into the enlisted men's barracks on Tuesday and stayed at the fort marking time because of Amy's request. For three long days, he hung around the barracks, checked over the horses, went through the equipment, and paid a brief daily call on Amy at the colonel's house.

Their visits were perfunctory. On Friday, he decided it was time to end the waiting. The sooner he stood face-to-face with Benjamin Travis, the better.

"I've decided to head out tomorrow morning," he said as soon as Mrs. Munroe had left him and Amy in the sitting room.

"But. . ." Her blue eyes showed plainly that she was disappointed.

"I might as well go. I'm not doing anyone any good here. If things have cleared up, I'll report to your father, then go home. If they still need help, well, I'll be where I'm needed."

"Are you able to travel so far?"

He moved his injured shoulder self-consciously. "I'm fine. A little stiff, but the doctor says I ought to use it."

"I'm glad."

"I've decided to keep the bay horse. He's the only one that didn't try to run off on me."

"He seems like a good horse. Have you named him?"

Tom shook his head. Horses' names were the last thing occupying him at the moment.

"You ought to name him Milton," Amy said with a smile. *"They also serve who only stand and wait."*

Tom tried to smile, but it was more of a grimace. He couldn't feel lighthearted. "I came to see if you want anything from the gear."

Amy shook her head.

"All right. I gave one of the muskets to Mike. I'll sell the pinto and the brown horse and give you half the money."

Her eyebrows shot up. "Don't give me anything."

"It will help toward your trip."

"My trip?"

"Back to Albany."

She caught her breath. "That's all right. Father will take care of me."

Like I failed to do, Tom thought. He stood up and walked to the window.

"Tom, take me with you."

He stood motionless, looking out at the parade ground, his heart racing. No, he certainly could not take her with him. One wild ride across hostile territory with Amy Travis was enough for the toughest man. He knew he couldn't survive it again. His heart would give out on him before he reached the Sweetwater. And he had yet to report to her father.

"The major wants you here," he said.

He heard her step toward him. "I want to go back, and Father said I might if it's safe."

Safe. There it was again.

He turned slowly. "Amy, I think I've already proven I'm not able to keep you safe. Major Travis told me to bring you here. I don't think he'd appreciate it if I took you back into danger."

She frowned and opened her mouth as if to argue, but at that moment Mrs. Munroe stepped into the doorway.

"Excuse me, Amy, but my husband just sent a man to tell us that your father is on his way here."

"He's coming here?" Amy faced her, astonished.

"Yes, they say he'll be here tomorrow. He sent a man ahead

to tell the colonel. The Indian threat is over, and he wants to meet my husband and discuss some military matters with him, then take you back to Fort Bridger himself."

Tom watched Amy. She was excited, happy. Her eyes sparkled the way they had before Independence Rock.

Mrs. Munroe left them, and Amy smiled at him.

"Tom, he's coming here! Isn't that wonderful? And I can go back!"

He picked his hat up from the sofa. "Maybe I'll head out today."

"Today?" she cried in dismay. "But he'll be here tomorrow."

He turned the hat slowly. "If he's that close, I can ride out to his camp tonight, see him there, and then go home."

"But—"

"I ought to get back to my place." It was an excuse, but he couldn't confess to the major, then travel all the way back with them. Travis wouldn't want him along, and Tom would be nervous, not to mention having to look at Amy. He'd lectured himself sternly several times, reminding himself that he was not and never would be on an equal plane with Amy. But his heart seemed to forget that when he saw her. It thumped disconcertingly, and he ached to hold her in his arms again.

Her father would take applications for suitors from stronger men than T. R. Barkley. Someone who could *really* take care of his daughter. Tom thought it might take a general with a brigade at his command to protect Amy Travis. In the stress of their flight from the outlaws, he had allowed himself to love her, but even then he had known there was no future for them.

"Maybe I'll see you at Bridger sometime," he muttered. She said nothing, and he pushed past her, clapping the hat on, trying to avoid her eyes. If she was going to cry again, he didn't want to know it.

seventeen

The major and his men were bivouacked near the ferry on the Platte. With every step the bay horse took away from Fort Laramie, Tom's heart sank lower. He knew he would avoid seeing Amy when she returned to Bridger.

He came to the camp after dark, and Major Travis came toward him from the tents.

"Barkley!" He grasped his hand. "Didn't expect you."

"Well, sir, I heard you were on the way, and I was anxious to get back to my place——"

Travis nodded. "Come, give me the full story. I've only heard bits and pieces."

Tom dropped the bay's reins and walked beside Travis away from the camp.

"Things are settled at Bridger?" he asked.

"Yes. It was a near thing. They gathered two thousand strong after you left, and I was a bit worried."

"Did they attack?"

"Yes, but we did pretty well. I had two men wounded, but we hit at least a dozen of them. They backed off. Wouldn't parlay. I was afraid they'd come back again, and I didn't know as we could hold out. Our defenses are really pretty flimsy."

Tom nodded.

"Then—what do you think?"

"I have no idea, sir."

"Old Jim Bridger himself came riding in on a mule. Once the Indians heard he was there, they agreed to talk. The entire matter was settled within hours, and they dispersed. Bridger said he'd stick around for a few weeks, and I thought it was safe to come retrieve my daughter."

"She's very anxious to see you, sir."

"Your brother, Private Barkley, said he'd seen her. I was a bit anxious about her. I got a note that worried me from that ruffian LeBeau, but I'm told you and Amy got through all right."

Tom cleared his throat. Travis was eyeing him keenly. "She did have some injuries, sir. I'm sorry. I'd like to give you my report if I may."

"Of course. Tell me everything."

They walked along the bluff for half an hour, and Tom held nothing back. When Tom finished, Travis stood with his hands behind his back, looking down on the river.

"I owe you and Brown a great debt."

"No, sir. It was a matter of duty."

"Perhaps, but—"

"I want to apologize, sir, for not keeping her safe."

Travis looked at him curiously. "But she's with Colonel Munroe. You said so yourself."

"Yes, sir, but I mean. . ." Tom turned his hat in his hands nervously. "That night, on the hill—I ought to have done something different, sir. Got her back quicker. I–I don't really know how much she suffered that night. I'm sorry." He stared down at the ground.

Travis watched the river and said slowly, "You can't go on fretting about the past, Barkley. Every time I give an order, I wonder if I've made the right decision. But you can only do your best at the time and keep going. I don't fault you for the way you handled things."

"Yes, sir." Tom stood, feeling miserable.

"That's leadership. You act, and you take the consequences. I picked you because I figured you could do that and because you know this stretch of trail better than just about anyone. Was I wrong?"

"No, sir." Tom knew he could bear the weight of responsibility for the mission, but he still felt a bittersweet regret when he remembered the time he had spent with Amy.

Travis looked up at the star-filled sky. "You came here to report to me sooner than you had to tonight. I'm wondering if this whole thing hasn't been weighing on you disproportionately."

"Sir?"

"Forget about me for a minute, son. Ultimately, we all stand before God. Can you say in your heart that you did your best? That you took what God gave you to work with and used it to the best of your ability to accomplish His purpose as far as you understood it?"

Tom went over the pursuit again in his mind and took a deep breath.

"Don't answer me," said the major. "Tell your heavenly Father. If you honestly believe you acted the way He wanted you to, then you have nothing to be ashamed of and nothing to fear from me or from God."

Tom stood silent. He wished he could have done better, yet. . .

Lord, I did what I could that night. Thank You for bringing us out of it. Without You, I couldn't have done it. Thank You.

Travis turned and surveyed Tom thoughtfully. "Do you have feelings for my daughter, Barkley?"

Tom was startled. "I. . .well. . ." He cleared his throat. "Yes, sir, I admit I do, but I want you to know I tried to treat her with utmost respect, and I know you would never approve—" He stopped helplessly. "You don't have to worry, sir," he finished, meeting the major's eyes.

Travis held the gaze for several seconds, and Tom breathed deeply, forcing himself to stand still and take it.

"I would never approve?"

Tom opened his mouth, then closed it.

"Come back to the campfire with me, Barkley. You can spend a little time with your brother tonight, and there's something I think you ought to see."

Tom's heart began to pound. Had they found some trace of the battle or Layton's body?

As they walked, Major Travis said affably, "My daughter has a stubborn streak. Don't know as you noticed that."

Tom grunted. "Yes, sir. She saved my neck when I'd told her not to."

Travis laughed. "Yes, well, I want you to look at this. Captain Hollis brought it to me at Fort Bridger."

Beside the fire, the major pulled a sheet of paper from his uniform pocket and handed it over. Tom opened it curiously and held it down where he could read it by the light of the flames.

Dearest Father,

I write this hastily to tell you that I am safe at Fort Laramie, thanks to Mr. T. R. Barkley and Pvt. Michael Brown. Although we had a difficult journey and Pvt. Layton was killed on the way, we have arrived, and it is to these two brave men that I owe my life. I hope you can do something for Pvt. Brown, as he hopes to go back to his family soon.

Father, I was badly frightened, and I spent a rather woeful night in the company of the vilest sort of man, but I stress to you that, other than a few bruises, I was not harmed, and you must not let this affect your treatment of his brother, Raymond LeBeau.

It is with deepest sincerity that I beg you not to send me back to Albany. I have come to care deeply for Mr. Barkley, and I cannot leave the Wyoming territory unless I know for certain that he will never reciprocate. He is very ill now because of the wound he received for my sake, and I am afraid for him. My heart tells me I can never love another man the way I do Tom Barkley. Please do not send me away.

Your loving daughter,
Amy

Tom looked up slowly.

"Well?" Travis asked. "I told you, she's stubborn."

Tom swallowed. "I don't know what to say, sir. It's a relief—I mean, the first part. But I wasn't trying to put notions in her head. I'm sorry."

She still loved him, and she had told her father! His heart raced. If the major sent him angrily away, he would still have that.

Travis said gently, "You go on back to the Black Fork if you want, Barkley, but I'm hoping you'll see fit to turn around and ride back to Fort Laramie with me in the morning."

"Are you saying you wouldn't object if I. . ." Tom swallowed hard. "If I courted your daughter?"

"I'd be most disappointed if you didn't."

๛

Amy was waiting anxiously with Colonel and Mrs. Munroe when her father's party rode into Fort Laramie at midmorning. They halted on the parade ground, and her father dismounted and dismissed the troops, handing the reins of his horse to his aide.

He walked toward her, smiling, and she ran to him, throwing her arms around his neck.

"Father! I'm so glad to see you!"

He kissed her cheek and held her at arm's length. "I heard the story from Barkley last night. Are you all right?"

"Yes. Oh, Father, did he apologize and tell you he didn't do his job?"

Travis laughed. "You seem to know Barkley pretty well. The way he tells it, he owes his life to you and that gray horse of mine."

"But Tom was wonderful. He outsmarted that awful man, and—"

Her father held up his hands in protest. "Let's discuss it inside, Amy."

She glanced around and blushed, realizing that the colonel,

his wife, and several other spectators were listening eagerly.

❧

Tom watched from a distance. He caught his breath when he saw Amy fly into her father's arms. She was lovely, her golden hair braided and wound on top of her head. She wore an impractical white dress that skimmed her ankles above the leather boots. He watched her go inside with the major, then he turned his horse out with Kip and headed for the barracks, meeting Brown outside the door.

"T.R.! You came back with the major?"

"He asked me to."

Brown was wary. "We're not in trouble, are we?"

"No. He's going to give you a commendation. And Mike, he gave me his blessing."

"You mean—Amy?"

"Yes." Tom gulped. "What do I say to her?"

Brown laughed. "You'll think of something."

"Well, if she'll have me—"

"I don't think there's much doubt of that. But last night I thought you'd ruined everything."

"Really?"

"Yes. I went by to see her, and she was taking it hard that you left."

"I felt like I had to, Mike. If I'd stayed. . . Well, I figured it was better to be a hundred miles or so away when the major told her I wasn't eligible."

Brown shook his head. "Don't know how you could walk out on those blue eyes. She cried buckets on my uniform."

"What did you tell her?"

"That you weren't uncaring, just knot-headed."

"Oh, I care, Mike."

"I know. But she was finding that hard to believe."

Colonel Munroe's aide approached them. "Private Brown? Mr. Barkley? You're wanted in headquarters."

"Time to make my report, I guess," said Brown.

Tom walked with him to the colonel's office. When they entered, Munroe and Travis were deep in discussion.

"Come in, Brown," said the colonel, glancing up. "I'd like you to give the major your version of the engagement at Independence Rock."

Travis looked at Tom. "Barkley, my daughter would like to see you. I believe she's with Mrs. Munroe."

Tom backed out the door and slowly went the few steps to the commander's quarters and knocked. The colonel's wife opened the door.

"Mr. Barkley! Welcome! Won't you come in? Miss Travis is—"

"Thank you," Tom murmured, walking past her into the sitting room. Amy jumped up from a chair and stood facing him, her hands twisting the ends of a blue sash the same color as her eyes.

"Tom!" There was a hesitance in her manner as she greeted him. "Father told me he brought you back, and I ought to talk to you."

He advanced slowly toward her, his hat in his hands. She reached out toward him, then drew her hands back uncertainly.

He walked closer and stood just inches from her, unsure how to begin.

"Tom, if I offended you somehow on the trail. . .I mean, it seems looking back that I may have been indiscreet, and. . . I'm sorry!" Her eyes pleaded for understanding.

He put his left hand up and rested his index finger lightly on her lips. "Shh. Do you still want to go with me?"

The gladness that filled her face was intoxicating. "Of course!"

"I love you, Amy. Didn't get a chance to tell you before I fell off the horse."

She caught her breath, and he was afraid she was going to cry. He let his fingers stroke her cheek. He smiled faintly. "Guess you found some of that lard."

Her eyes flared, then she laughed. He let his hat fall to the floor and drew her into his arms slowly but purposefully. He brought his lips down tenderly on hers, and she melted against him, her hands creeping up onto his shoulders.

"I plan to leave in the morning," he whispered in her ear, holding her close against his thudding heart.

"But Father said he'll be here three days."

"I know. Thought we'd go alone. It ought to be safe with troopers back and forth so much right now."

She drew back quickly and stared at him. "Just you and me?"

He nodded. "We can get married tonight. What do you say? There's a chaplain here, and you could wear that dress. You look beautiful, Amy."

She gasped. "But, Tom, you'll have to ask Father. I mean, he told me he respects you, but—"

"I had that talk with him last night. He'll give us his approval, Amy. Please, will you be my wife?"

Her smile started deep in her eyes and spread to her lips.

"Can we stop at Jim Frye's cabin?"

Tom laughed. "All right, but this time the horses stay outside."

"Yes, and we'll take extra clothes and blankets and some decent food. I'd better tell Mrs. Munroe. Maybe she and I can bake this afternoon. And we ought to have a tent in case we get caught in the rain again."

"Sounds like I'd better line up a pack horse." Tom laughed at her enthusiasm and the joy that was shooting through him.

She caught her breath. "Oh, and can we take a few books? The trader has some."

"You start baking and packing. I'll go see to our gear." He looked down into her eyes, smiling, not loosening his hold on her. "Still love me?"

Amy sighed contentedly. "Always."

A Letter To Our Readers

Dear Reader:

In order that we might better contribute to your reading enjoyment, we would appreciate your taking a few minutes to respond to the following questions. We welcome your comments and read each form and letter we receive. When completed, please return to the following:

Fiction Editor
Heartsong Presents
PO Box 719
Uhrichsville, Ohio 44683

1. Did you enjoy reading *Protecting Amy* by Susan Page Davis?
   ❑ Very much! I would like to see more books by this author!
   ❑ Moderately. I would have enjoyed it more if

   _____

   _____

   _____

2. Are you a member of **Heartsong Presents**? ❑ Yes ❑ No
   If no, where did you purchase this book? _____

   _____

3. How would you rate, on a scale from 1 (poor) to 5 (superior), the cover design? _____

4. On a scale from 1 (poor) to 10 (superior), please rate the following elements.

   ____ Heroine   ____ Plot
   ____ Hero   ____ Inspirational theme
   ____ Setting   ____ Secondary characters

5. These characters were special because?_____
   _____
   _____

6. How has this book inspired your life?_____
   _____
   _____

7. What settings would you like to see covered in future
   Heartsong Presents books? _____
   _____
   _____

8. What are some inspirational themes you would like to see
   treated in future books? _____
   _____
   _____

9. Would you be interested in reading other **Heartsong
   Presents** titles? ❏ Yes ❏ No

10. Please check your age range:
    ❏ Under 18   ❏ 18-24
    ❏ 25-34   ❏ 35-45
    ❏ 46-55   ❏ Over 55

Name_____
Occupation _____
Address _____
City_____ State_____ Zip_____